Tales of Long Ago

Arthur Conan Doyle

ALMA CLASSICS

ALMA CLASSICS LTD
Hogarth House
32–34 Paradise Road
Richmond
Surrey TW9 1SE
United Kingdom
www.almaclassics.com

Tales of Long Ago first published in 1922
This edition first published by Alma Classics Ltd in 2015

Cover image © Marina Rodrigues

Printed and bound by CPI Group (UK) Ltd, Croydon, CR0 4YY

ISBN: 978-1-84749-410-8

Contents

Tales of Long Ago

The Last of the Legions

P ONTUS, THE ROMAN VICEROY, sat in the atrium of his palatial villa by the Thames, and he looked with perplexity at the scroll of papyrus which he had just unrolled. Before him stood the messenger who had brought it, a swarthy little Italian, whose black eyes were glazed with want of sleep, and his olive features darker still from dust and sweat. The Viceroy was looking fixedly at him, yet he saw him not, so full was his mind of this sudden and most unexpected order. To him it seemed as if the solid earth had given way beneath his feet. His life and the work of his life had come to irremediable ruin.

"Very good," he said at last in a hard dry voice, "you can go."

The man saluted and staggered out of the hall. A yellow-haired British major-domo came forward for orders.

"Is the General there?"

"He is waiting, Your Excellency."

"Then show him in, and leave us together."

A few minutes later Licinius Crassus, the head of the British military establishment, had joined his chief. He was a large, bearded man in a white civilian toga, hemmed with the patrician purple. His rough, bold features, burnt and seamed and lined with the long African wars, were shadowed with anxiety as he looked with questioning eyes at the drawn, haggard face of the Viceroy.

"I fear, Your Excellency, that you have had bad news from Rome."

"The worst, Crassus. It is all over with Britain. It is a question whether even Gaul will be held."

"St Albus save us! Are the orders precise?"

"Here they are, with the Emperor's own seal."

"But why? I had heard a rumour, but it had seemed too incredible."

"So had I only last week, and had the fellow scourged for having spread it. But here it is as clear as words can make it: 'Bring every man of the legions by forced marches to the help of the empire. Leave not a cohort in Britain.' These are my orders."

"But the cause?"

"They will let the limbs wither so that the heart be stronger. The old German hive is about to swarm once more. There are fresh crowds of barbarians from Dacia and Scythia. Every sword is needed to hold the Alpine passes. They cannot let three legions lie idle in Britain."

The soldier shrugged his shoulders.

"When the legions go no Roman would feel that his life was safe here. For all that we have done, it is nonetheless the truth that it is no country of ours, and that we hold it as we won it by the sword."

"Yes, every man, woman and child of Latin blood must come with us to Gaul. The galleys are already waiting at Portus Dubris.* Get the orders out, Crassus, at once. As the Valerian legion falls back from the Wall of Hadrian* it can take the northern colonists with it. The Jovians can bring in the people from the west, and the Batavians can escort the easterns if they will muster at Camboricum.* You will see to it." He sank his face for a moment in his hands. "It is a fearsome thing," said he, "to tear up the roots of so goodly a tree."

"To make more space for such a crop of weeds," said the soldier bitterly. "My God, what will be the end of these poor Britons! From ocean to ocean there is not a tribe which will not be at the throat of its neighbour when the last Roman lictor has turned his back. With these hot-headed Silures* it is hard enough now to keep the swords in their sheaths."

"The kennel might fight as they choose among themselves until the best hound won," said the Roman Governor. "At least the victor would keep the arts and the religion which we have brought them, and Britain would be one land. No, it is the bear from the north and the wolves from oversea, the painted savage from beyond the walls and the Saxon pirate from over the water, who will succeed to our rule. Where we saved, they will slay; where we built, they will burn; where we planted, they will ravage. But the die is cast, Crassus. You will carry out the orders."

"I will send out the messengers within an hour. This very morning there has come news that the barbarians are through the old gap in the wall, and their outriders as far south as Vinovia."*

The Governor shrugged his shoulders.

"These things concern us no longer," said he. Then a bitter smile broke upon his aquiline clean-shaven face. "Whom think you that I see in audience this morning?"

"Nay, I know not."

"Caradoc and Regnus, and Celticus the Icenian,* who, like so many of the richer Britons, have been educated at Rome, and who would lay before me their plans as to the ruling of this country."

"And what is their plan?"

"That they themselves should do it."

The Roman soldier laughed. "Well, they will have their will," said he, as he saluted and turned upon his heel. "Farewell, Your Excellency. There are hard days coming for you and for me."

An hour later the British deputation was ushered into the presence of the Governor. They were good, steadfast men, men who with a whole heart, and at some risk to themselves, had taken up their country's cause, so far as they could see it. At the same time they well knew that under the mild and beneficent rule of Rome it was only when they passed from words to deeds that their backs or their necks would be in danger. They stood now, earnest and a little abashed, before the throne of the Viceroy. Celticus was a swarthy, black-bearded little Iberian. Caradoc and Regnus were tall, middle-aged men of the fair, flaxen British type. All three were dressed in the draped yellow toga after the Latin fashion, instead of in the *bracæ** and tunic which distinguished their more insular fellow countrymen.

"Well?" asked the Governor.

"We are here," said Celticus boldly, "as the spokesmen of a great number of our fellow countrymen, for the purpose of sending our petition through you to the Emperor and to the Roman Senate, that we may urge upon them the policy of allowing us to govern this country after our own ancient fashion." He paused, as if awaiting some outburst as an answer to his own temerity; but the Governor merely nodded his head as a sign that he should proceed. "We had laws of our own before ever Caesar set foot in Britain, which have served their purpose since first our forefathers came from the land of Ham.* We are not a child among the nations, but our history goes back in our own traditions further even than that of Rome, and we are galled by this yoke which you have laid upon us."

"Are not our laws just?" asked the Governor.

"The code of Caesar is just, but it is always the code of Caesar. Our own laws were made for our own uses and our own circumstances, and we would fain have them again."

"You speak Roman as if you had been bred in the Forum; you wear a Roman toga; your hair is filleted in Roman fashion – are not these the gifts of Rome?"

"We would take all the learning and all the arts that Rome or Greece could give, but we would still be Britain, and ruled by Britons."

The Viceroy smiled. "By the rood of St Helena," said he, "had you spoken thus to some of my heathen ancestors, there would have been an end to your politics. That you have dared to stand before my face and say as much is a proof for ever of the gentleness of our rule. But I would reason with you for a moment upon this your request. You know well that this land has never been one kingdom, but was always under many chiefs and many tribes, who have made war upon each other. Would you in very truth have it so again?"

"Those were in the evil pagan days, the days of the Druid and the oak grove, Your Excellency. But now we are held together by a gospel of peace."

The Viceroy shook his head. "If all the world were of the same way of thinking, then it would be easier," said he. "It may be that this blessed doctrine of peace will be little help to you when you are face to face with strong men who still worship the god of war. What would you do against the Picts* of the north?"

"Your Excellency knows that many of the bravest legionaries are of British blood. These are our defence."

"But discipline, man, the power to command, the knowledge of war, the strength to act – it is in these things that you would fail. Too long have you leant upon the crutch."

"The times may be hard, but when we have gone through them, Britain will be herself again."

"Nay, she will be under a different and a harsher master," said the Roman. "Already the pirates swarm upon the eastern coast. Were it not for our Roman Count of the Saxon Shore* they would land tomorrow. I see the day when Britain may, indeed, be one; but that will be because you and your fellows are either dead or are driven into the mountains of the west. All goes into the melting pot, and if a better Albion should come forth from it, it will be after ages of strife, and neither you nor your people will have part or lot in it."

Regnus, the tall young Celt, smiled. "With the help of God and our own right arms we should hope for a better end," said he. "Give us but the chance, and we will bear the brunt."

"You are as men that are lost," said the Viceroy sadly. "I see this broad land, with its gardens and orchards, its fair villas and its walled towns, its bridges and its roads, all the work of Rome. Surely it will pass even as a dream, and these three hundred years of settled order will leave no trace behind. For learn that it will indeed be as you wish, and that this very day the orders have come to me that the legions are to go."

The three Britons looked at each other in amazement. Their first impulse was towards a wild exultation, but reflection and doubt followed close upon its heels.

"This is indeed wondrous news," said Celticus. "This is a day of days to the motherland. When do the legions go, Your Excellency, and what troops will remain behind for our protection?"

"The legions go at once," said the Viceroy. "You will doubtless rejoice to hear that within a month there will be no Roman soldier in the island, nor, indeed, a Roman of any sort, age or sex, if I can take them with me."

The faces of the Britons were shadowed, and Caradoc, a grave and thoughtful man, spoke for the first time.

"But this is over-sudden, Your Excellency," said he. "There is much truth in what you have said about the pirates. From my villa near the fort of Anderida* I saw eighty of their galleys only last week, and I know well that they would be on us like ravens on a dying ox. For many years to come it would not be possible for us to hold them off."

The Viceroy shrugged his shoulders. "It is your affair now," said he. "Rome must look to herself."

The last traces of joy had passed from the faces of the Britons. Suddenly the future had started up clearly before them, and they quailed at the prospect.

"There is a rumour in the marketplace," said Celticus, "that the northern barbarians are through the gap in the wall. Who is to stop their progress?"

"You and your fellows," said the Roman.

Clearer still grew the future, and there was terror in the eyes of the spokesmen as they faced it.

"But, Your Excellency, if the legions should go at once, we should have the wild Scots at York, and the Northmen* in the Thames within the month. We can build ourselves up under your shield, and in a few years it would be easier for us; but not now, Your Excellency, not now."

"Tut, man; for years you have been clamouring in our ears and raising the people. Now you have got what you asked. What more would you have? Within the month you will be as free as were your ancestors before Caesar set foot upon your shore."

"For God's sake, Your Excellency, put our words out of your head. The matter had not been well considered. We will send to Rome. We will ride post-haste ourselves. We will fall at the Emperor's feet. We will kneel before the Senate and beg that the legions remain."

The Roman proconsul rose from his chair and motioned that the audience was at an end.

"You will do what you please," said he. "I and my men are for Italy."

And even as he said, so was it, for before the spring had ripened into summer, the troops were clanking down the Via Aurelia on their way to the Ligurian passes,* whilst every road in Gaul was dotted with the carts and the wagons which bore the Brito-Roman refugees on their weary journey to their distant country. But ere another summer had passed Celticus was dead, for he was flayed alive by the pirates and his skin nailed upon the door of a church near Caistor.* Regnus, too, was dead, for he was tied to a tree and shot with arrows when the painted men came to the sacking of Isca.* Caradoc only was alive, but he was a slave to Elda the red Caledonian and his wife was mistress to Mordred the wild chief of the western Cymri. From the ruined wall in the north to Vectis* in the south blood and ruin and ashes covered the fair land of Britain. And after many days it came out fairer than ever, but, even as the Roman had said, neither the Britons nor any men of their blood came into the heritage of that which had been their own.

The Last Galley

Mutato nomine, de te, Britannia,
*fabula narratur.**

I T WAS A SPRING MORNING, 146 years before the coming
of Christ. The North African coast, with its broad hem
of golden sand, its green belt of feathery palm trees and its
background of barren, red-scarped hills, shimmered like a
dream country in the opal light. Save for a narrow edge of
snow-white surf, the Mediterranean lay blue and serene as
far as the eye could reach. In all its vast expanse there was
no break but for a single galley, which was slowly making its
way from the direction of Sicily and heading for the distant
harbour of Carthage.*

Seen from afar it was a stately and beautiful vessel, deep
red in colour, double-banked with scarlet oars, its broad,
flapping sail stained with Tyrian purple,* its bulwarks
gleaming with brass work. A brazen, three-pronged ram
projected in front, and a high golden figure of Baal, the
god of the Phoenicians, children of Canaan, shone upon
the afterdeck. From the single high mast above the huge sail
streamed the tiger-striped flag of Carthage. So, like some
stately scarlet bird, with golden beak and wings of purple,

she swam upon the face of the waters – a thing of might and of beauty as seen from the distant shore.

But approach and look at her now! What are these dark streaks which foul her white decks and dapple her brazen shields? Why do the long red oars move out of time, irregular, convulsive? Why are some missing from the staring portholes, some snapped with jagged, yellow edges, some trailing inert against the side? Why are two prongs of the brazen ram twisted and broken? See, even the high image of Baal is battered and disfigured! By every sign this ship has passed through some grievous trial, some day of terror, which has left its heavy marks upon her.

And now stand upon the deck itself, and see more closely the men who man her! There are two decks forward and aft, while in the open waist are the double banks of seats, above and below, where the rowers, two to an oar, tug and bend at their endless task. Down the centre is a narrow platform, along which pace a line of warders, lash in hand, who cut cruelly at the slave who pauses, be it only for an instant, to sweep the sweat from his dripping brow. But these slaves – look at them! Some are captured Romans, some Sicilians, many black Libyans, but all are in the last exhaustion, their weary eyelids drooped over their eyes, their lips thick with black crusts, and pink with bloody froth, their arms and backs moving mechanically to the hoarse chant of the overseer. Their bodies of all tints from ivory to jet, are stripped to the waist, and every glistening back shows the angry stripes of the warders. But it is not from these that the blood comes which reddens the seats and tints the salt water washing beneath their manacled feet. Great gaping wounds, the marks of sword slash and spear stab, show crimson upon their naked chests and shoulders, while many lie huddled and senseless athwart the benches, careless for ever of the whips which still hiss above them. Now we can understand those empty portholes and those trailing oars.

Nor were the crew in better case than their men to rouse the public spirit and waken the public conscience to the ever-increasing danger from Rome. As they talked, the two men glanced continually, with earnest anxious faces, towards the northern skyline.

"It is certain," said the older man, with gloom in his voice and bearing, "none have escaped save ourselves."

"I did not leave the press of the battle whilst I saw one ship which I could succour," Magro answered. "As it was, we came away, as you saw, like a wolf which has a hound hanging on to either haunch. The Roman dogs can show the wolf bites which prove it. Had any other galley won clear, they would surely be with us by now, since they have no place of safety save Carthage."

The younger warrior glanced keenly ahead to the distant point which marked his native city. Already the low, leafy hill could be seen, dotted with the white villas of the wealthy Phoenician merchants. Above them, a gleaming dot against the pale-blue morning sky, shone the brazen roof of the citadel of Byrsa, which capped the sloping town.

"Already they can see us from the watchtowers," he remarked. "Even from afar they may know the galley of Black Magro. But which of all of them will guess that we alone remain of all that goodly fleet which sailed out with blare of trumpet and roll of drum but one short month ago?"

The patrician smiled bitterly. "If it were not for our great ancestors and for our beloved country, the Queen of the Waters,"* said he, "I could find it in my heart to be glad at this destruction which has come upon this vain and feeble generation. You have spent your life upon the seas, Magro. You do not know how it has been with us on the land. But I have seen this canker grow upon us which now leads us to our death. I and others have gone down into the marketplace to plead with the people, and been pelted with mud for our pains. Many a time have I pointed to Rome, and said, 'Behold these people, who bear arms themselves, each man for his own duty and pride. How can you who hide behind mercenaries hope to stand against them?' A hundred times I have said it."

"And had they no answer?" asked the rover.

"Rome was far off and they could not see it, so to them it was nothing," the old man answered. "Some thought of trade, and some of votes, and some of profits from the state, but none would see that the state itself, the mother of all things, was sinking to her end. So might the bees debate who should have wax or honey when the torch was blazing which would bring to ashes the hive and all therein. 'Are we not rulers of the sea?' 'Was not Hannibal a great man?' Such were their cries, living ever in the past and blind to the future. Before that sun sets there will be tearing of hair and rending of garments; but what will that now avail us?"

"It is some sad comfort," said Magro, "to know that what Rome holds she cannot keep."

"Why say you that? When we go down, she is supreme in all the world."

"For a time, and only for a time," Magro answered gravely. "Yet you will smile, perchance, when I tell you how it is that I know it. There was a wise woman who lived in that part of the Tin Islands* which juts forth into the sea, and from her lips I have heard many things, but not one which has not come aright. Of the fall of our own country, and even of this battle, from which we now return, she told me clearly. There is much strange lore amongst these savage peoples in the west of the land of Tin."

"What said she of Rome?"

"That she also would fall, even as we, weakened by her riches and her factions."

Gisco rubbed his hands. "That at least makes our own fall less bitter," said he. "But since we have fallen, and Rome will fall, who in turn may hope to be Queen of the Waters?"

"That also I asked her," said Magro, "and gave her my Tyrian belt with the golden buckle as a guerdon for her answer. But, indeed, it was too high payment for the tale she told, which must be false if all else she said was true. She would have it that in coming days it was her own land, this fog-girt isle where painted savages can scarce row a wicker coracle from point to point, which shall at last take the trident which Carthage and Rome have dropped."

The smile which flickered upon the old patrician's keen features died away suddenly, and his fingers closed upon his companion's wrist. The other had set rigid, his head advanced, his hawk eyes upon the northern skyline. Its straight, blue horizon was broken by two low black dots.

"Galleys!" whispered Gisco.

The whole crew had seen them. They clustered along the starboard bulwarks, pointing and chattering. For a moment the gloom of defeat was lifted, and a buzz of joy ran from group to group at the thought that they were not alone – that someone had escaped the great carnage as well as themselves.

"By the spirit of Baal," said Black Magro, "I could not have believed that any could have fought clear from such a welter. Could it be young Hamilcar in the *Africa*, or is it Beneva in the blue Syrian ship? We three with others may form a squadron and make head against them yet. If we hold our course, they will join us ere we round the harbour mole."

Slowly the injured galley toiled on her way, and more swiftly the two newcomers swept down from the north. Only a few miles off lay the green point and the white houses which flanked the great African city. Already, upon the headland, could be seen a dark group of waiting townsmen. Gisco and Magro were still watching with puckered gaze the approaching galleys, when the brown Libyan boatswain, with flashing teeth and gleaming eyes, rushed upon the poop, his long thin arm stabbing to the north.

"Romans!" he cried. "Romans!"

A hush had fallen over the great vessel. Only the wash of the water and the measured rattle and beat of the oars broke in upon the silence.

"By the horns of God's altar, I believe the fellow is right!" cried old Gisco. "See how they swoop upon us like falcons. They are full-manned and full-oared."

"Plain wood, unpainted," said Magro. "See how it gleams yellow where the sun strikes it."

"And yonder thing beneath the mast. Is it not the cursed bridge they use for boarding?"

"So they grudge us even one," said Magro with a bitter laugh. "Not even one galley shall return to the old sea-mother. Well, for my part, I would as soon have it so. I am of a mind to stop the oars and await them."

"It is a man's thought," answered old Gisco. "But the city will need us in the days to come. What shall it profit us to make the Roman victory complete? Nay, Magro, let the slaves row as they never rowed before, not for our own safety, but for the profit of the state."

So the great red ship laboured and lurched onwards, like a weary panting stag which seeks shelter from his pursuers, while ever swifter and ever nearer sped the two lean, fierce galleys from the north. Already the morning sun shone upon the lines of low Roman helmets above the bulwarks, and glistened on the silver wave where each sharp prow shot through the still blue water. Every moment the ships drew nearer, and the long thin scream of the Roman trumpets grew louder upon the ear.

Upon the high bluff of Megara* there stood a great concourse of the people of Carthage who had hurried forth from the city upon the news that the galleys were in sight.

They stood now, rich and poor, effete and plebeian, white Phoenician and dark Kabyle,* gazing with breathless interest at the spectacle before them. Some hundreds of feet beneath them the Punic* galley had drawn so close that with their naked eyes they could see those stains of battle which told their dismal tale. The Romans, too, were heading in such a way that it was before their very faces that their ship was about to be cut off; and yet of all this multitude not one could raise a hand in its defence. Some wept in impotent grief, some cursed with flashing eyes and knotted fists, some on their knees held up appealing hands to Baal; but neither prayer, tears nor curses could undo the past nor mend the present. That broken, crawling galley meant that their fleet was gone. Those two fierce, darting ships meant that the hands of Rome were already at their throat. Behind them would come others and others, the innumerable trained hosts of the great Republic, long mistress of the land, now dominant also upon the waters. In a month, two months, three at the most, their armies would be there, and what could all the untrained multitudes of Carthage do to stop them?

"Nay!" cried one, more hopeful than the rest. "At least we are brave men with arms in our hands."

"Fool!" said another. "Is it not such talk which has brought us to our ruin? What is the brave man untrained to the brave man trained? When you stand before the sweep and rush of a Roman legion you may learn the difference."

"Then let us train!"

"Too late! A full year is needful to turn a man to a soldier. Where will you – where will your city be within the year? Nay, there is but one chance for us. If we give up our commerce and our colonies, if we strip ourselves of all that made us great, then perchance the Roman conqueror may hold his hand."

And already the last sea fight of Carthage was coming swiftly to an end before them. Under their very eyes the two Roman galleys had shot in, one on either side of the vessel of Black Magro. They had grappled with him, and he, desperate in his despair, had cast the crooked flukes of his anchors over their gunwales, and bound them to him in an iron grip, whilst with hammer and crowbar he burst great holes in his own sheathing. The last Punic galley should never be rowed into Ostia,* a sight for the holidaymakers of Rome. She would lie in her own waters. And the fierce, dark soul of her rover captain glowed as he thought that not alone should she sink into the depths of the mother sea.

Too late did the Romans understand the man with whom they had to deal. Their boarders who had flooded the Punic decks felt the planking sink and sway beneath them. They rushed to gain their own vessels; but they, too, were being drawn downwards, held in the dying grip of the great red galley. Over they went and ever over. Now the deck of Magro's ship is flush with the water, and the Romans', drawn towards it by the iron bonds which hold them, are tilted downwards, one bulwark upon the waves, one reared high in the air. Madly they strain to cast off the death grip of the galley. She is under the surface now, and ever swifter, with the greater weight, the Roman ships heel after her. There is a rending crash. The wooden side is torn out of one, and mutilated, dismembered, she rights herself, and lies a helpless thing upon the water. But a last yellow gleam in the blue water shows where her consort has been dragged to her end in the iron death grapple of her foeman. The tiger-striped flag of Carthage has sunk beneath the swirling surface, never more to be seen upon the face of the sea.

For in that year a great cloud hung for seventeen days over the African coast, a deep black cloud which was the dark shroud of the burning city. And when the seventeen days were over, Roman ploughs were driven from end to end of the charred ashes, and salt was scattered there as a sign that Carthage should be no more. And far off a huddle of naked, starving folk stood upon the distant mountains, and looked down upon the desolate plain which had once been the fairest and richest upon earth. And they understood too late that it is the law of heaven that the world is given to the hardy and to the self-denying, whilst he who would escape the duties of manhood will soon be stripped of the pride, the wealth and the power, which are the prizes which manhood brings.

Through the Veil

H E WAS A GREAT SHOCK-HEADED, freckle-faced Borderer,* the lineal descendant of a cattle-thieving clan in Liddesdale. In spite of his ancestry he was as solid and sober a citizen as one would wish to see, a town council-lor of Melrose, an elder of the Church and the chairman of the local branch of the Young Men's Christian Association. Brown was his name – and you saw it printed up as "Brown and Handiside" over the great grocery stores in the High Street. His wife, Maggie Brown, was an Armstrong before her marriage, and came from an old farming stock in the wilds of Teviothead. She was small, swarthy and dark-eyed, with a strangely nervous temperament for a Scotch woman. No greater contrast could be found than the big tawny man and the dark little woman, but both were of the soil as far back as any memory could extend.

One day – it was the first anniversary of their wedding – they had driven over together to see the excavations of the Roman fort at Newstead. It was not a particularly pic-turesque spot. From the northern bank of the Tweed, just where the river forms a loop, there extends a gentle slope of arable land. Across it run the trenches of the excavators, with here and there an exposure of old stonework to show the foundations of the ancient walls. It had been a huge place, for the camp was fifty acres in extent, and the fort fifteen. However, it was all made easy for them since Mr Brown knew the farmer to whom the land belonged. Under his guidance they spent a long summer evening inspecting the trenches, the pits, the ramparts and all the strange variety of objects which were waiting to be transported to the Edinburgh Museum of Antiquities. The buckle of a woman's belt had been dug up that very day, and the farmer was discoursing upon it when his eyes fell upon Mrs Brown's face.

"Your good leddy's tired," said he. "Maybe you'd best rest a wee before we gang further."

Brown looked at his wife. She was certainly very pale, and her dark eyes were bright and wild.

"What is it, Maggie? I've wearied you. I'm thinkin' it's time we went back."

"No, no, John, let us go on. It's wonderful! It's like a dreamland place. It all seems so close and so near to me. How long were the Romans here, Mr Cunningham?"

"A fair time, mam. If you saw the kitchen midden pits you would guess it took a long time to fill them."

"And why did they leave?"

"Well, mam, by all accounts they left because they had to. The folk round could thole* them no longer, so they just up and burned the fort aboot their lugs.* You can see the fire marks on the stanes."

The woman gave a quick little shudder. "A wild night – a fearsome night," said she. "The sky must have been red that night – and these grey stones, they may have been red also."

"Aye, I think they were red," said her husband. "It's a queer thing, Maggie, and it may be your words that have done it; but I seem to see that business aboot as clear as ever I saw anything in my life. The light shone on the water."

"Aye, the light shone on the water. And the smoke gripped you by the throat. And all the savages were yelling."

The old farmer began to laugh. "The leddy will be writin' a story aboot the old fort," said he. "I've shown many a one ower it, but I never heard it put so clear afore. Some folk have the gift."

They had strolled along the edge of the fosse,* and a pit yawned upon the right of them.

"That pit was fourteen foot deep," said the farmer. "What d'ye think we dug oot from the bottom o't? Weel, it was just the skeleton of a man wi' a spear by his side. I'm thinkin' he was grippin' it when he died. Now, how cam' a man wi' a spear doon a hole fourteen foot deep? He wasna' buried there, for they aye burned their dead. What make ye o' that, mam?"

"He sprang doon to get clear of the savages," said the woman.

"Weel, it's likely enough, and a' the professors from Edinburgh couldna gie a better reason. I wish you were aye here, mam, to answer a' oor deeficulties sae readily. Now, here's the altar that we foond last week. There's an inscreeption. They tell me it's Latin, and it means that the men o' this fort give thanks to God for their safety."

They examined the old worn stone. There was a large, deeply cut "VV" upon the top of it.

"What does 'VV' stand for?" asked Brown.

"Naebody kens," the guide answered.

"*Valeria Victrix*,"* said the lady softly. Her face was paler than ever, her eyes far away, as one who peers down the dim aisles of overarching centuries.

"What's that?" asked her husband sharply.

She started as one who wakes from sleep. "What were we talking about?" she asked.

"About this 'VV' upon the stone."

"No doubt it was just the name of the legion which put the altar up."

"Aye, but you gave some special name."

"Did I? How absurd! How should I ken what the name was?"

"You said something – '*Victrix*', I think."

"I suppose I was guessing. It gives me the queerest feeling, this place, as if I were not myself, but someone else."

"Aye, it's an uncanny place," said her husband, looking round with an expression almost of fear in his bold grey eyes. "I feel it mysel'. I think we'll just be wishin' you good evenin', Mr Cunningham, and get back to Melrose before the dark sets in."

Neither of them could shake off the strange impression which had been left upon them by their visit to the excavations. It was as if some miasma had risen from those damp trenches and passed into their blood. All the evening they were silent and thoughtful, but such remarks as they did make showed that the same subject was in the mind of each. Brown had a restless night, in which he dreamt a strange connected dream, so vivid that he woke sweating and shivering like a frightened horse. He tried to convey it all to his wife as they sat together at breakfast in the morning.

"It was the clearest thing, Maggie," said he. "Nothing that has ever come to me in my waking life has been more clear than that. I feel as if these hands were sticky with blood."

"Tell me of it – tell me slow," said she.

"When it began, I was oot on a braeside. I was laying flat on the ground. It was rough, and there were clumps of heather. All round me was just darkness, but I could hear the rustle and the breathin' of men. There seemed a great multitude on every side of me, but I could see no one. There was a low chink of steel sometimes, and then a number of voices would whisper 'Hush!' I had a ragged club in my hand, and it had spikes o' iron near the end of it. My heart was beatin' quickly, and I felt that a moment of great danger and excitement was at hand. Once I dropped my club, and again from all round me the voices in the darkness cried, 'Hush!' I put oot my hand, and it touched the foot of another man lying in front of me. There was someone at my very elbow on either side. But they said nothin'.

"Then we all began to move. The whole braeside seemed to be crawlin' downwards. There was a river at the bottom and a high-arched wooden bridge. Beyond the bridge were many lights – torches on a wall. The creepin' men all flowed towards the bridge. There had been no sound of any kind, just a velvet stillness. And then there was a cry in the darkness, the cry of a man who had been stabbed suddenly to the hairt. That one cry swelled out for a moment, and then the roar of a thoosand furious voices. I was runnin'. Everyone was runnin'. A bright-red light shone out, and the river was a scarlet streak. I could see my companions now. They were more like devils than men, wild figures clad in skins, with their hair and beards streamin'. They were all mad with rage, jumpin' as they ran, their mouths open, their arms wavin', the red light beatin' on their faces. I ran, too, and yelled out curses like the rest. Then I heard a great cracklin' of wood, and I knew that the palisades were doon. There was a loud whistlin' in my ears, and I was aware that arrows were flyin' past me. I got to the bottom of a dyke, and I saw a hand stretched doon from above. I took it, and was dragged to the top. We looked doon, and there were silver men beneath us holdin' up their spears. Some of our folk sprang on to the spears. Then we others followed, and we killed the soldiers before they could draw the spears oot again. They shouted loud in some foreign tongue, but no mercy was shown them. We went ower them like a wave, and trampled them doon into the mud, for they were few, and there was no end to our numbers.

"I found myself among buildings, and one of them was on fire. I saw the flames spoutin' through the roof. I ran on, and then I was alone among the buildings. Someone ran across in front o' me. It was a woman. I caught her by the arm, and I took her chin and turned her face so as the light of the fire would strike it. Whom think you that it was, Maggie?"

His wife moistened her dry lips. "It was I," she said.

He looked at her in surprise. "That's a good guess," said he. "Yes, it was just you. Not merely like you, you understand. It was you – you yourself. I saw the same soul in your frightened eyes. You looked white and bonnie and wonderful in the firelight. I had just one thought in my head – to get you awa' with me; to keep you all to mysel' in my own home somewhere beyond the hills. You clawed at my face with your nails. I heaved you over my shoulder, and I tried to find a way oot of the light of the burning hoose and back into the darkness.

"Then came the thing that I mind best of all. You're ill, Maggie. Shall I stop? My God! You have the very look on your face that you had last night in my dream. You screamed. He came runnin' in the firelight. His head was bare; his hair was black and curled; he had a naked sword in his hand, short and broad, little more than a dagger. He stabbed at me, but he tripped and fell. I held you with one hand, and with the other—"

His wife had sprung to her feet with writhing features.

"Marcus!" she cried. "My beautiful Marcus! Oh, you brute! You brute! You brute!" There was a clatter of teacups as she fell forward senseless upon the table.

They never talk about that strange isolated incident in their married life. For an instant the curtain of the past had

34

swung aside, and some strange glimpse of a forgotten life had come to them. But it closed down, never to open again. They live their narrow round – he in his shop, she in her household – and yet new and wider horizons have vaguely formed themselves around them since that summer evening by the crumbling Roman fort.

The Coming of the Huns

IN THE MIDDLE OF THE FOURTH CENTURY the state of the Christian religion was a scandal and a disgrace. Patient, humble and long-suffering in adversity, it had become positive, aggressive and unreasonable with success. Paganism was not yet dead, but it was rapidly sinking, finding its most faithful supporters among the conservative aristocrats of the best families on the one hand, and among those benighted villagers on the other who gave their name to the expiring creed. Between these two extremes the great majority of reasonable men had turned from the conception of many gods to that of one, and had rejected for ever the beliefs of their forefathers. But with the vices of polytheism, they had also abandoned its virtues, among which toleration and religious good humour had been conspicuous. The strenuous earnestness of the Christians had compelled them to examine and define every point of their own theology; but as they had no central authority by which such definitions could be checked, it was not long before a hundred heresies had put forward their rival views, while the same earnestness of conviction led the stronger bands of schismatics to endeavour, for conscience sake, to force their views upon the weaker, and thus to cover the Eastern world with confusion and strife.

Alexandria, Antioch and Constantinople were centres of theological warfare. The whole north of Africa, too, was rent by the strife of the Donatists,* who upheld their particular schism by iron flails and the war cry of "Praise to the Lord!" But minor local controversies sank to nothing when compared with the huge argument of the Catholic and the Arian,* which rent every village in twain, and divided every household from the cottage to the palace. The rival doctrines of the Homoousian and of the Homoiousian,* containing metaphysical differences so attenuated that they could hardly be stated, turned bishop against bishop and congregation against congregation. The ink of the theologians and the blood of the fanatics were spilt in floods on either side, and gentle followers of Christ were horrified to find that their faith was responsible for such a state of riot and bloodshed as had never yet disgraced the religious history of the world. Many of the more earnest among them, shocked and scandalized, slipped away to the Libyan Desert, or to the solitude of Pontus,* there to await in self-denial and prayer that second coming which was supposed to be at hand. Even in the deserts they could not escape the echo of the distant strife, and the hermits themselves scowled fiercely from their dens at passing travellers who might be contaminated by the doctrines of Athanasius* or of Arius.

Such a hermit was Simon Melas, of whom I write. A Trinitarian and a Catholic, he was shocked by the excesses of the persecution of the Arians, which could be only matched by the similar outrages with which these same Arians in the day of their power avenged their treatment on their brother Christians. Weary of the whole strife, and convinced that the end of the world was indeed at hand, he left his home in Constantinople and travelled as far as the Gothic settlements in Dacia, beyond the Danube, in search of some spot where he might be free from the never-ending disputes. Still journeying to the north and east, he crossed the river which we now call the Dniester,* and there, finding a rocky hill rising from an immense plain, he formed a cell near its summit, and settled himself down to end his life in self-denial and meditation. There were fish in the stream, the country teemed with game, and there was an abundance of wild fruits, so that his spiritual exercises were not unduly interrupted by the search of sustenance for his mortal frame.

In this distant retreat he expected to find absolute solitude, but the hope was in vain. Within a week of his arrival, in an hour of worldly curiosity, he explored the edges of the high rocky hill upon which he lived. Making his way up to a cleft, which was hung with olives and myrtles, he came upon a cave in the opening of which sat an aged man, white-bearded, white-haired and infirm – a hermit like himself. So long had this stranger been alone that he had almost forgotten the use of his tongue; but at last, words coming more freely, he was able to convey the information that his name was Paul of Nicopolis, that he was a Greek citizen, and that he also had come out into the desert for the saving of his soul, and to escape from the contamination of heresy.

"Little I thought, brother Simon," said he, "that I should ever find anyone else who had come so far upon the same holy errand. In all these years, and they are so many that I have lost count of them, I have never seen a man, save indeed one or two wandering shepherds far out upon yonder plain."

From where they sat, the huge steppe, covered with waving grass and gleaming with a vivid green in the sun, stretched away as level and as unbroken as the sea, to the eastern horizon. Simon Melas stared across it with curiosity.

"Tell me, brother Paul," said he, "you who have lived here so long – what lies at the farther side of that plain?"

The old man shook his head. "There is no farther side to the plain," said he. "It is the earth's boundary, and stretches away to eternity. For all these years I have sat beside it, but never once have I seen anything come across it. It is manifest that if there had been a farther side there would certainly at some time have come some traveller from that direction.

Over the great river yonder is the Roman post of Tyras;* but that is a long day's journey from here, and they have never disturbed my meditations."

"On what do you meditate, brother Paul?"

"At first I meditated on many sacred mysteries; but now, for twenty years, I have brooded continually on the nature of the Logos.* What is your view upon that vital matter, brother Simon?"

"Surely," said the younger man, "there can be no question as to that. The Logos is assuredly but a name used by St John to signify the Deity." The old hermit gave a hoarse cry of fury, and his brown, withered face was convulsed with anger. Seizing the huge cudgel which he kept to beat off the wolves, he shook it murderously at his companion.

"Out with you! Out of my cell!" he cried. "Have I lived here so long to have it polluted by a vile Trinitarian – a follower of the rascal Athanasius? Wretched idolater, learn once for all, that the Logos is in truth an emanation from the Deity, and in no sense equal or coeternal with Him! Out with you, I say, or I will dash out your brains with my staff!"

It was useless to reason with the furious Arian, and Simon withdrew in sadness and wonder, that at this extreme verge of the known earth the spirit of religious strife should still break upon the peaceful solitude of the wilderness. With hanging head and heavy heart he made his way down the valley, and climbed up once more to his own cell, which lay at the crown of the hill, with the intention of never again exchanging visits with his Arian neighbour.

Here, for a year, dwelt Simon Melas, leading a life of solitude and prayer. There was no reason why anyone should ever come to this outermost point of human habitation. Once, a young Roman officer – Caius Crassus – rode out a day's journey from Tyras, and climbed the hill to have speech with the anchorite. He was of an equestrian family, and still held his belief in the old dispensation. He looked with interest and surprise, but also with some disgust, at the ascetic arrangements of that humble abode.

"Whom do you please by living in such a fashion?" he asked.

"We show that our spirit is superior to our flesh," Simon answered. "If we fare badly in this world, we believe that we shall reap an advantage in the world to come."

The centurion shrugged his shoulders. "There are philosophers among our people, Stoics and others, who have the same idea. When I was in the Herulian Cohort of the Fourth Legion we were quartered in Rome itself, and I saw much of the Christians, but I could never learn anything from them which I had not heard from my own father, whom you, in your arrogance, would call a pagan. It is true that we talk of numerous gods; but for many years we have not taken them very seriously. Our thoughts upon virtue and duty and a noble life are the same as your own."

Simon Melas shook his head.

"If you have not the holy books," said he, "then what guide have you to direct your steps?"

"If you will read our philosophers, and above all the divine Plato, you will find that there are other guides who may take you to the same end. Have you by chance read the book which was written by our Emperor Marcus Aurelius?* Do you not discover there every virtue which man could have, although he knew nothing of your creed? Have you considered, also, the words and actions of our late Emperor Julian,* with whom I served my first campaign when he went out against the Persians? Where could you find a more perfect man than he?"

"Such talk is unprofitable, and I will have no more of it," said Simon sternly. "Take heed while there is time, and embrace the true faith; for the end of the world is at hand, and when it comes there will be no mercy for those who have shut their eyes to the light." So saying, he turned back once more to his praying stool and to his crucifix, while the young Roman walked in deep thought down the hill and, mounting his horse, rode off to his distant post. Simon watched him until his brazen helmet was but a bead of light on the western edge of the great plain; for this was the first human face that he had seen in all this long year, and there were times when his heart yearned for the voices and the faces of his kind.

So another year passed, and save for the change of weather and the slow change of the seasons, one day was as another. Every morning when Simon opened his eyes, he saw the same grey line ripening into red in the farthest east, until the bright rim pushed itself above that far-off horizon across which no living creature had ever been known to come. Slowly the sun swept across the huge arch of the heavens, and as the shadows shifted from the black rocks which jutted upward from above his cell, so did the hermit regulate his terms of prayer and meditation. There was nothing on earth to draw his eye, or to distract his mind, for the grassy plain below was as void from month to month as the heaven above. So the long hours passed, until the red rim slipped down on the farther side, and the day ended in the same pearl-grey shimmer with which it had begun. Once two ravens circled for some days round the lonely hill, and once a white fish eagle came from the Dniester and screamed above the hermit's head. Sometimes red dots were seen on the green plain where the antelopes grazed, and often a wolf howled in the darkness from the base of the rocks. Such was the uneventful life of Simon Melas the anchorite, until there came the day of wrath.

It was in the late spring of the year 375 that Simon came out from his cell, his gourd in his hand, to draw water from the spring. Darkness had closed in, the sun had set, but one last glimmer of rosy light rested upon a rocky peak, which jutted forth from the hill, on the farther side from the hermit's dwelling. As Simon came forth from under his ledge, the gourd dropped from his hand, and he stood gazing in amazement.

On the opposite peak a man was standing, his outline black in the fading light. He was a strange, almost a deformed figure, short-statured, round-backed, with a large head, no neck, and a long rod jutting out from between his shoulders. He stood with his face advanced, and his body bent, peering very intently over the plain to the westward. In a moment he was gone, and the lonely black peak showed up hard and naked against the faint eastern glimmer. Then the night closed down, and all was black once more.

Simon Melas stood long in bewilderment, wondering who this stranger could be. He had heard, as had every Christian, of those evil spirits which were wont to haunt the hermits in the Thebaid and on the skirts of the Ethiopian waste. The strange shape of this solitary creature, its dark outline and prowling, intent attitude, suggestive rather of a fierce, rapacious beast than of a man, all helped him to believe that he had at last encountered one of those wanderers from the pit, of whose existence, in those days of robust faith, he had no more doubt than of his own. Much of the night he spent in prayer, his eyes glancing continually at the low arch of his cell door, with its curtain of deep purple wrought with stars. At any instant some crouching monster, some horned abomination, might peer in upon him, and he clung with frenzied appeal to his crucifix, as his human weakness quailed at the thought. But at last his fatigue overcame his fears, and falling upon his couch of dried grass, he slept until the bright daylight brought him to his senses.

It was later than was his wont, and the sun was far above the horizon. As he came forth from his cell, he looked across at the peak of rock, but it stood there bare and silent. Already it seemed to him that that strange dark figure which had startled him so was some dream, some vision of the twilight. His gourd lay where it had fallen, and he picked it up with the intention of going to the spring. But suddenly he was aware of something new. The whole air was throbbing with sound. From all sides it came, rumbling, indefinite, an inarticulate mutter, low, but thick and strong, rising, falling, reverberating among the rocks, dying away into vague whispers, but always there. He looked round at the blue, cloudless sky in bewilderment. Then he scrambled up the rocky pinnacle above him, and sheltering himself in its shadow, he stared out over the plain. In his wildest dream he had never imagined such a sight.

The whole vast expanse was covered with horsemen, hundreds and thousands and tens of thousands, all riding slowly and in silence, out of the unknown east. It was the multitudinous beat of their horses' hoofs which caused that low throbbing in his ears. Some were so close to him as he looked down upon them that he could see clearly their thin, wiry horses, and the strange humped figures of their swarthy riders, sitting forward on the withers, shapeless bundles, their short legs hanging stirrupless, their bodies balanced as firmly as though they were part of the beast. In those nearest he could see the bow and the quiver, the long spear and the short sword, with the coiled lasso behind the rider, which told that this was no helpless horde of wanderers, but a formidable army upon the march. His eyes passed on from them and swept farther and farther, but still to the very horizon, which quivered with movement, there was no end to this monstrous cavalry. Already the vanguard was far past the island of rock upon which he dwelt, and he could now understand that in front of this vanguard were single scouts who guided the course of the army, and that it was one of these whom he had seen the evening before.

All day, held spellbound by this wonderful sight, the hermit crouched in the shadow of the rocks, and all day the sea of horsemen rolled onward over the plain beneath. Simon had seen the swarming quays of Alexandria, he had watched the mob which blocked the hippodrome of Constantinople, yet never had he imagined such a multitude as now defiled beneath his eyes, coming from that eastern skyline which had been the end of his world. Sometimes the dense streams of horsemen were broken by droves of brood mares and foals, driven along by mounted guards; sometimes there were herds of cattle; sometimes there were lines of wagons with skin canopies above them; but then once more, after every break, came the horsemen, the horsemen, the hundreds and the thousands and the tens of thousands, slowly, ceaselessly, silently drifting from the east to the west. The long day passed, the light waned, and the shadows fell, but still the great broad stream was flowing by.

But the night brought a new and even stranger sight. Simon had marked bundles of faggots upon the backs of many of the led horses, and now he saw their use. All over the great plain, red pinpoints gleamed through the darkness, which grew and brightened into flickering columns of flame. So far as he could see both to east and west the fires extended, until they were but points of light in the farthest distance. White stars shone in the vast heavens above, red ones in the great plain below. And from every side rose the low, confused murmur of voices, with the lowing of oxen and the neighing of horses.

Simon had been a soldier and a man of affairs before ever he forsook the world, and the meaning of all that he had seen was clear to him. History told him how the Roman world had ever been assailed by fresh swarms of barbarians, coming from the outer darkness, and that the eastern empire had already, in its fifty years of existence since Constantine had moved the capital of the world to the shores of the Bosphorus,* been tormented in the same way. Gepidae and Heruli, Ostrogoths and Sarmatians, he was familiar with them all. What the advanced sentinel of Europe had seen from this lonely outlying hill, was a fresh swarm breaking in upon the empire, distinguished only from the others by its enormous, incredible size and by the strange aspect of the warriors who composed it. He alone of all civilized men knew of the approach of this dreadful shadow, sweeping like a heavy storm cloud from the unknown depths of the east. He thought of the little Roman posts along the Dniester, of the ruined Dacian wall of Trajan behind them, and then of the scattered, defenceless villages which lay with no thought of danger over all the open country which stretched down to the Danube. Could he but give them the alarm! Was it not, perhaps, for that very end that God had guided him to the wilderness?

Then suddenly he remembered his Arian neighbour, who dwelt in the cave beneath him. Once or twice during the last year he had caught a glimpse of his tall, bent figure hobbling round to examine the traps which he laid for quails and partridges. On one occasion they had met at the brook; but the old theologian waved him away as if he were a leper. What did he think now of this strange happening? Surely their differences might be forgotten at such a moment. He stole down the side of the hill, and made his way to his fellow hermit's cave.

But there was a terrible silence as he approached it. His heart sank at that deadly stillness in the little valley. No glimmer of light came from the cleft in the rocks. He entered and called, but no answer came back. Then, with flint, steel and the dry grass which he used for tinder, he struck a spark, and blew it into a blaze. The old hermit, his white hair dabbled with crimson, lay sprawling across the floor. The broken crucifix, with which his head had been beaten in, lay in splinters across him. Simon had dropped on his knees beside him, straightening his contorted limbs, and muttering the office for the dead, when the thud of a horse's hoofs was heard ascending the little valley which led to the hermit's cell. The dry grass had burnt down, and Simon crouched trembling in the darkness, pattering prayers to the Virgin that his strength might be upheld.

It may have been that the newcomer had seen the gleam of the light, or it may have been that he had heard from his comrades of the old man whom they had murdered, and that his curiosity had led him to the spot. He stopped his horse outside the cave, and Simon, lurking in the shadows within, had a fair view of him in the moonlight. He slipped from his saddle, fastened the bridle to a root, and then stood peering through the opening of the cell. He was a very short, thick man, with a dark face, which was gashed with three cuts upon either side. His small eyes were sunk deep in his head, showing like black holes in the heavy, flat, hairless face. His legs were short and very bandy, so that he waddled uncouthly as he walked.

Simon crouched in the darkest angle, and he gripped in his hand that same knotted cudgel which the dead theologian had once raised against him. As that hideous stooping head advanced into the darkness of the cell, he brought the staff down upon it with all the strength of his right arm, and then, as the stricken savage fell forward upon his face, he struck madly again and again, until the shapeless figure lay limp and still. One roof covered the first slain of Europe and of Asia.

Simon's veins were throbbing and quivering with the unwonted joy of action. All the energy stored up in those years of repose came in a flood at this moment of need.

Standing in the darkness of the cell, he saw, as in a map of fire, the outlines of the great barbaric host, the line of the river, the position of the settlements, the means by which they might be warned. Silently he waited in the shadow until the moon had sunk. Then he flung himself upon the dead man's horse, guided it down the gorge, and set forth at a gallop across the plain.

There were fires on every side of him, but he kept clear of the rings of light. Round each he could see, as he passed, the circle of sleeping warriors, with the long lines of picketed horses. Mile after mile and league after league stretched that huge encampment. And then, at last, he had reached the open plain which led to the river, and the fires of the invaders were but a dull smoulder against the black eastern sky. Ever faster and faster he sped across the steppe, like a single fluttered leaf which whirls before the storm. Even as the dawn whitened the sky behind him, it gleamed also upon the broad river in front, and he flogged his weary horse through the shallows, until he plunged into its full yellow tide.

So it was that, as the young Roman centurion – Caius Crassus – made his morning round in the fort of Tyras he saw a single horseman, who rode towards him from the river. Weary and spent, drenched with water and caked with dirt and sweat, both horse and man were at the last stage of their endurance. With amazement the Roman watched their progress, and recognized in the ragged, swaying figure, with flying hair and staring eyes, the hermit of the eastern desert. He ran to meet him, and caught him in his arms as he reeled from the saddle.

"What is it, then?" he asked. "What is your news?"

But the hermit could only point at the rising sun. "To arms!" he croaked. "To arms! The day of wrath is come!" And as he looked, the Roman saw – far across the river – a great dark shadow, which moved slowly over the distant plain.

The Contest

I N THE YEAR OF OUR LORD 66, the Emperor Nero, being at that time in the twenty-ninth year of his life and the thirteenth of his reign, set sail for Greece with the strangest company and the most singular design that any monarch has ever entertained.* With ten galleys he went forth from Puteoli,* carrying with him great stores of painted scenery and theatrical properties, together with a number of knights and senators, whom he feared to leave behind him at Rome, and who were all marked for death in the course of his wanderings. In his train he took Natus, his singing coach; Cluvius, a man with a monstrous voice, who should bawl out his titles; and a thousand trained youths who had learnt to applaud in unison whenever their master sang or played in public. So deftly had they been taught that each had his own role to play. Some did no more than give forth a low deep hum of speechless appreciation. Some clapped with enthusiasm. Some, rising from approbation into absolute frenzy, shrieked, stamped and beat sticks upon the benches. Some – and they were the most effective – had learnt from an Alexandrian a long droning musical note which they all uttered together, so that it boomed over the assembly. With the aid of these mercenary admirers, Nero had every hope, in spite of his indifferent voice and clumsy execution, to return to Rome, bearing with him the chaplets for song offered for free competition by the Greek cities. As his great gilded galley with two tiers of oars passed down the Mediterranean, the Emperor sat in his cabin all day, his teacher by his side, rehearsing from morning to night those compositions which he had selected, whilst every few hours a Nubian slave massaged the Imperial throat with oil and balsam, that it might be ready for the great ordeal which lay before it in the land of poetry and song. His food, his drink and his exercise were prescribed for him as for an athlete who trains for a contest, and the twanging of his lyre, with the strident notes of his voice, resounded continually from the Imperial quarters.

Now it chanced that there lived in those days a Grecian goatherd named Policles, who tended and partly owned a great flock which grazed upon the long flanks of the hills near Heroea, which is five miles north of the river Alpheus, and no great distance from the famous Olympia. This person was noted over all the countryside as a man of strange gifts and singular character. He was a poet who had twice been crowned for his verses, and he was a musician to whom the use and sound of an instrument were so natural that one would more easily meet him without his staff than his harp. Even in his lonely vigils on the winter hills he would bear it always slung over his shoulder, and would pass the long hours by its aid, so that it had come to be part of his very self. He was beautiful also, swarthy and eager, with a head like Adonis, and in strength there was no one who could compete with him. But all was ruined by his disposition, which was so masterful that he would brook no opposition nor contradiction. For this reason he was continually at enmity with all his neighbours, and in his fits of temper he would spend months at a time in his stone hut among the mountains, hearing nothing from the world, and living only for his music and his goats.

One spring morning, in the year of 67, Policies, with the aid of his boy Dorus, had driven his goats over to a new pasturage which overlooked from afar the town of Olympia. Gazing down upon it from the mountain, the shepherd was surprised to see that a portion of the famous amphitheatre had been roofed in, as though some performance was being enacted. Living far from the world and from all news, Policies could not imagine what was afoot, for he was well aware that the Grecian games were not due for two years to come. Surely some poetic or musical contest must be proceeding of which he had heard nothing. If so, there would perhaps be some chance of his gaining the votes of the judges; and in any case he loved to hear the compositions and admire the execution of the great minstrels who assembled on such an occasion. Calling to Dorus, therefore, he left the goats to his charge, and strode swiftly away, his harp upon his back, to see what was going forward in the town.

When Policies came into the suburbs, he found them deserted; but he was still more surprised when he reached the main street to see no single human being in the place. He hastened his steps, therefore, and as he approached the theatre he was conscious of a low sustained hum which announced the concourse of a huge assembly. Never in all his dreams had he imagined any musical competition upon so vast a scale as this. There were some soldiers clustering outside the door; but Policies pushed his way swiftly through them, and found himself upon the outskirts of the multitude who filled the great space formed by roofing over a portion of the national stadium. Looking around him, Policies saw a great number of his neighbours, whom he knew by sight, tightly packed upon the benches, all with their eyes fixed upon the stage. He also observed that there were soldiers round the walls, and that a considerable part of the hall was filled by a body of youths of foreign aspect, with white gowns and long hair. All this he perceived; but what it meant he could not imagine. He bent over to a neighbour to ask him, but a soldier prodded him at once with the butt end of his spear, and commanded him fiercely to hold his peace. The man whom he had addressed, thinking that Policles had demanded a seat, pressed closer to his neighbour, and so the shepherd found himself sitting at the end of the bench which was nearest to the door. Thence he concentrated himself upon the stage, on which Metas, a well-known minstrel from Corinth and an old friend of Policles, was singing and playing without much encouragement from the audience. To Policles it seemed that Metas was having less than his due, so he applauded loudly, but he was surprised to observe that the soldiers frowned at him, and that all his neighbours regarded him with some surprise. Being a man of strong and obstinate character, he was the more inclined to persevere in his clapping when he perceived that the general sentiment was against him.

But what followed filled the shepherd poet with absolute amazement. When Metas of Corinth had made his bow and withdrawn to half-hearted and perfunctory applause, there appeared upon the stage, amid the wildest enthusiasm upon the part of the audience, a most extraordinary figure. He was a short fat man, neither old nor young, with a bull neck and a round, heavy face, which hung in creases in front like the dewlap of an ox. He was absurdly clad in a short blue tunic, braced at the waist with a golden belt. His neck and part of his chest were exposed, and his short, fat legs were bare from the buskins below to the middle of his thighs, which was as far as his tunic extended. In his hair were two golden wings, and the same upon his heels, after the fashion of the god Mercury. Behind him walked a Negro bearing a harp, and beside him a richly dressed officer who bore rolls of music. This strange creature took the harp from the hands of the attendant, and advanced to the front of the stage, whence he bowed and smiled to the cheering audience. "This is some foppish singer from Athens," thought Policies to himself, but at the same time he understood that only a great master of song could receive such a reception from a Greek audience. This was evidently some wonderful performer whose reputation had preceded him. Policies settled down, therefore, and prepared to give his soul up to the music.

The blue-clad player struck several chords upon his lyre, and then burst suddenly out into the 'Ode of Niobe'. Policies sat straight up on his bench and gazed at the stage in amazement. The tune demanded a rapid transition from a low note to a high, and had been purposely chosen for this reason. The low note was a grunting, a rumble, the deep discordant growling of an ill-conditioned dog. Then suddenly the singer threw up his face, straightened his tubby figure, rose upon his tiptoes, and with wagging head and scarlet cheeks emitted such a howl as the same dog might have given had his growl been checked by a kick from his master. All the while the lyre twanged and thrummed, sometimes in front of and sometimes behind the voice of the singer. But what amazed Policies most of all was the effect of this performance upon the audience. Every Greek was a trained critic, and as unsparing in his hisses as he was lavish in his applause. Many a singer far better than this absurd fop had been driven amid execration and abuse from the platform. But now, as the man stopped and wiped the abundant sweat from his fat face, the whole assembly burst into a delirium of appreciation. The shepherd held his hands to his bursting head, and felt that his reason must be leaving him. It was surely a dreadful musical nightmare, and he would wake soon and laugh at the remembrance. But no; the figures were real, the faces were those of his neighbours, the cheers which resounded in his ears were indeed from an audience which filled the theatre of Olympia. The whole chorus was in full blast, the hummers humming, the shouters bellowing, the tappers hard at work upon the benches, while every now and then came a musical cyclone of "Incomparable! Divine!" from the trained phalanx who intoned their applause, their united voices sweeping over the tumult as the drone of the wind dominates the roar of the sea. It was madness – insufferable madness! If this were allowed to pass, there was an end of all musical justice in Greece. Policies's conscience would not permit him to be still. Standing upon his bench with waving hands and upraised voice, he protested with all the strength of his lungs against the mad judgement of the audience.

At first, amid the tumult, his action was hardly noticed. His voice was drowned in the universal roar which broke out afresh at each bow and smirk from the fatuous musician. But gradually the folk round Policles ceased clapping, and stared at him in astonishment. The silence grew in ever widening circles, until the whole great assembly sat mute, staring at this wild and magnificent creature who was storming at them from his perch near the door.

"Fools!" he cried. "What are you clapping at? What are you cheering? Is this what you call music? Is this cat-calling to earn an Olympian prize? The fellow has not a note in his voice. You are either deaf or mad, and I for one cry shame upon you for your folly." Soldiers ran to pull him down, and the whole audience was in confusion, some of the bolder cheering the sentiments of the shepherd, and others crying that he should be cast out of the building. Meanwhile the successful singer, having handed his lyre to his Negro attendant, was enquiring from those around him on the stage as to the cause of the uproar. Finally a herald with an enormously powerful voice stepped forward to the front, and proclaimed that if the foolish person at the back of the hall, who appeared to differ from the opinion of the rest of the audience, would come forward upon the platform, he might, if he dared, exhibit his own powers, and see if he could outdo the admirable and wonderful exhibition which they had just had the privilege of hearing.

Policies sprang readily to his feet at the challenge, and, the great company making way for him to pass, he found himself a minute later standing in his unkempt garb, with his frayed and weather-beaten harp in his hand, before the expectant crowd. He stood for a moment tightening a string here and slackening another there until his chords rang true. Then, amid a murmur of laughter and jeers from the Roman benches immediately before him, he began to sing.

He had prepared no composition, but he had trained himself to improvise, singing out of his heart for the joy of the music. He told of the land of Elis, beloved of Jupiter, in which they were gathered that day, of the great bare mountain slopes, of the swift shadows of the clouds, of the winding blue river, of the keen air of the uplands, of the chill of the evenings, and the beauties of earth and sky. It was all simple and childlike, but it went to the hearts of the Olympians, for it spoke of the land which they knew and loved. Yet when he at last dropped his hand, few of them dared to applaud, and their feeble voices were drowned by a storm of hisses and groans from his opponents. He shrank back in horror from so unusual a reception, and in an instant his blue-clad rival was in his place. If he had sung badly before, his performance now was inconceivable. His screams, his grunts, his discords and harsh jarring cacophonies were an outrage to the very name of music. And yet every time that he paused for breath or to wipe his streaming forehead a fresh thunder of applause came rolling back from the audience. Policies sank his face in his hands and prayed that he might not be insane. Then, when the dreadful performance ceased, and the uproar of admiration showed that the crown was certainly awarded to this impostor, a horror of the audience, a hatred of this race of fools and a craving for the peace and silence of the pastures mastered every feeling in his mind. He dashed through the mass of people waiting at the wings, and emerged in the open air. His old rival and friend Metas of Corinth was waiting there with an anxious face.

"Quick, Policies, quick!" he cried. "My pony is tethered behind yonder grove. A grey he is, with red trappings. Get you gone as hard as hoof will bear you, for if you are taken you will have no easy death."

"No easy death! What mean you, Metas? Who is the fellow?"

"Great Jupiter! Did you not know? Where have you lived? It is Nero the Emperor! Never would he pardon what you have said about his voice. Quick, man, quick, or the guards will be at your heels!"

An hour later the shepherd was well on his way to his mountain home, and about the same time the Emperor, having received the Chaplet of Olympia for the incomparable excellence of his performance, was making enquiries with a frowning brow as to who the insolent person might be who had dared to utter such contemptuous criticisms.

"Bring him to me here this instant," said he, "and let Marcus with his knife and branding iron be in attendance."

"If it please you, great Caesar," said Arsenius Platus, the officer of attendance, "the man cannot be found, and there are some very strange rumours flying about."

"Rumours!" cried the angry Nero. "What do you mean, Arsenius? I tell you that the fellow was an ignorant upstart with the bearing of a boor and the voice of a peacock. I tell you also that there are a good many who are as guilty as he among the people, for I heard them with my own ears raise cheers for him when he had sung his ridiculous ode. I have half a mind to burn their town about their ears so that they may remember my visit."

"It is not to be wondered at if he won their votes, Caesar," said the soldier, "for from what I hear it would have been no disgrace had you, even you, been conquered in this contest."

"I conquered! You are mad, Arsenius. What do you mean?"

"None know him, great Caesar! He came from the mountains, and he disappeared into the mountains. You marked the wildness and strange beauty of his face. It is whispered that for once the great god Pan has condescended to measure himself against a mortal."

The cloud cleared from Nero's brow. "Of course, Arsenius! You are right! No man would have dared to brave me so. What a story for Rome! Let the messenger leave this very night, Arsenius, to tell them how their Emperor has upheld their honour in Olympia this day."

The First Cargo

Ex ovo omnia.*

WHEN YOU LEFT BRITAIN with your legion, my dear Crassus, I promised that I would write to you from time to time when a messenger chanced to be going to Rome, and keep you informed as to anything of interest which might occur in this country. Personally, I am very glad that I remained behind when the troops and so many of our citizens left, for though the living is rough and the climate is infernal, still by dint of the three voyages which I have made for amber to the Baltic, and the excellent prices which I obtained for it here, I shall soon be in a position to retire, and to spend my old age under my own fig tree, or even perhaps to buy a small villa at Baiae or Posuoli, where I could get a good sun bath after the continued fogs of this accursed island. I picture myself on a little farm, and I read the *Georgics** as a preparation; but when I hear the rain falling and the wind howling, Italy seems very far away.

In my previous letter I let you know how things were going in this country. The poor folk, who had given up all soldiering during the centuries that we guarded them, are now perfectly helpless before these Picts and Scots, tattooed barbarians from the north, who overrun the whole country and do exactly what they please. So long as they kept to the north, the people in the south, who are the most numerous, and also the most civilized of the Britons, took no heed of them; but now the rascals have come as far as London, and the lazy folk in these parts have had to wake up. Vortigern,* the King, is useless for anything but drink or women, so he sent across to the Baltic to get over some of the north Germans, in the hope that they would come and help him. It is bad enough to have a bear in your house, but it does not seem to me to mend matters if you call in a pack of ferocious wolves as well. However, nothing better could be devised, so an invitation was sent and very promptly accepted. And it is here that your humble friend appears upon the scene. In the course of my amber trading I had learnt the Saxon speech, and so I was sent down in all haste to the Kentish shore that I might be there when our new allies came. I arrived there on the very day when their first vessel appeared, and it is of my adventures that I wish to tell you. It is perfectly clear to me that the landing of these warlike Germans in England will prove to be an event of historical importance, and so your inquisitive mind will not feel wearied if I treat the matter in some detail.

It was, then, upon the day of Mercury, immediately following the Feast of Our Blessed Lord's Ascension, that I found myself upon the south bank of the river Thames, at the point where it opens into a wide estuary. There is an island there named Thanet, which was the spot chosen for the landfall of our visitors. Sure enough, I had no sooner ridden up than there was a great red ship, the first as it seems of three, coming in under full sail. The white horse, which is the ensign of these rovers, was hanging from her topmast, and she appeared to be crowded with men. The sun was shining brightly, and the great scarlet ship, with snow-white sails and a line of gleaming shields slung over her side, made as fair a picture on that blue expanse as one would wish to see.

I pushed off at once in a boat, because it had been arranged that none of the Saxons should land until the King had come down to speak with their leaders. Presently I was under the ship, which had a gilded dragon in the bows, and a tier of oars along either side. As I looked up, there was a row of helmeted heads looking down at me, and among them I saw, to my great surprise and pleasure, that of Eric the Swart, with whom I do business at Venta* every year. He greeted me heartily when I reached the deck, and became at once my guide, friend and counsellor. This helped me greatly with these barbarians, for it is their nature that they are very cold and aloof unless one of their own number can vouch for you, after which they are very hearty and hospitable. Try as they will, they find it hard, however, to avoid a certain suggestion of condescension, and in the baser sort, of contempt, when they are dealing with a foreigner.

It was a great stroke of luck meeting Eric, for he was able to give me some idea of how things stood before I was shown into the presence of Kenna, the leader of this particular ship. The crew, as I learnt from him, was entirely made up of three tribes or families – those of Kenna, of Lanc and of Hasta. Each of these tribes gets its name by putting the letters "ing" after the name of the chief, so that the people on board would describe themselves as Kennings, Lancings and Hastings. I observed in the Baltic that the villages were named after the family who lived in them, each keeping to itself, so that I have no doubt that if these fellows get a footing on shore, we shall see settlements with names like these rising up among the British towns.

The greater part of the men were sturdy fellows with red, yellow or brown hair, mostly the latter. To my surprise, I saw several women among them. Eric, in answer to my question, explained that they always take their women with them so far as they can, and that instead of finding them an encumbrance as our Roman dames would be, they look upon them as helpmates and advisers. Of course, I remembered afterwards that our excellent and accurate Tacitus has remarked upon this characteristic of the Germans.* All laws in the tribes are decided by votes, and a vote has not yet been given to the women, but many are in favour of it, and it is thought that woman and man may soon have the same power in the state, though many of the women themselves are opposed to such an innovation. I observed to Eric that it was fortunate there were several women on board, as they could keep each other company; but he answered that the wives of chiefs had no desire to know the wives of the inferior officers, and that both of them combined against the more common women, so that any companionship was out of the question. He pointed as he spoke to Editha, the wife of Kenna, a red-faced, elderly woman, who walked among the others, her chin in the air, taking no more notice than if they did not exist.

Whilst I was talking to my friend Eric, a sudden altercation broke out upon the deck, and a great number of the men paused in their work, and flocked towards the spot with faces which showed that they were deeply interested in the matter. Eric and I pushed our way among the others, for I was very anxious to see as much as I could of the ways and manners of these barbarians. A quarrel had broken out about a child, a little blue-eyed fellow with curly yellow hair, who appeared to be greatly amused by the hubbub of which he was the cause. On one side of him stood a white-bearded old man, of very majestic aspect, who signified by his gestures that he claimed the lad for himself, while on the other was a thin, earnest, anxious person, who strongly objected to the boy being taken from him. Eric whispered in my ear that the old man was the tribal high priest, who was the official sacrificer to their great god Woden,* whilst the other was a man who took somewhat different views, not upon Woden, but upon the means by which he should be worshipped. The majority of the crew were on the side of the old priest; but a certain number, who liked greater liberty of worship, and to invent their own prayers instead of always repeating the official ones, followed the lead of the younger man. The difference was too deep and too old to be healed among the grown men, but each had a great desire to impress his view upon the children. This was the reason why these two were now so furious with each other, and the argument between them ran so high that several of their followers on either side had drawn the short saxes, or knives from which their name of Saxon is derived, when a burly, red-headed man pushed his way through the throng, and in a voice of thunder brought the controversy to an end.

"You priests, who argue about the things which no man can know, are more trouble aboard this ship than all the dangers of the sea," he cried. "Can you not be content with worshipping Woden, over which we are all agreed, and not make so much of those small points upon which we may differ? If there is all this fuss about the teaching of the children, then I shall forbid either of you to teach them, and they must be content with as much as they can learn from their mothers."

The two angry teachers walked away with discontented faces; and Kenna – for it was he who spoke – ordered that a whistle should be sounded, and that the crew should assemble. I was pleased with the free bearing of these people, for though this was their greatest chief, they showed none of the exaggerated respect which soldiers of a legion might show to the Praetor, but met him on a respectful equality, which showed how highly they rated their own manhood.

From our Roman standard, his remarks to his men would seem very wanting in eloquence, for there were no graces nor metaphors to be found in them, and yet they were short, strong and to the point. At any rate it was very clear that they were to the minds of his hearers. He began by reminding them that they had left their own country because the land was all taken up, and that there was no use returning there, since there was no place where they could dwell as free and independent men. This island of Britain was but sparsely inhabited, and there was a chance that every one of them would be able to found a home of his own.

"You, Whitta," he said, addressing some of them by name, "you will found a Whitting hame, and you, Bucka, we shall see you in a Bucking hame, where your children's and your children's children will bless you for the broad acres which your valour will have gained for them." There was no word of glory or of honour in his speech, but he said that he was aware that they would do their duty, on which they all struck their swords upon their shields so that the Britons on the beach could hear the clang. Then, his eyes falling upon me, he asked me whether I was the messenger from Vortigern, and on my answering, he bid me follow him into his cabin, where Lanc and Hasta, the other chiefs, were waiting for a council.

Picture me, then, my dear Crassus, in a very low-roofed cabin, with these three huge barbarians seated round me. Each was clad in some sort of saffron tunic, with a chain-mail shirt over it, and a helmet with the horns of oxen on the sides, laid upon the table before him. Like most of the Saxon chiefs, their beards were shaved, but they wore their hair long and their huge light-coloured moustaches drooped down on to their shoulders. They are gentle, slow and some-what heavy in their bearing, but I can well fancy that their fury is the more terrible when it does arise.

Their minds seem to be of a very practical and positive nature, for they at once began to ask me a series of question

74

upon the numbers of the Britons, the resources of the kingdom, the conditions of its trade, and other such subjects. They then set to work arguing over the information which I had given, and became so absorbed in their own contention that I believe there were times when they forgot my presence. Everything, after due discussion, was decided between them by the vote, the one who found himself in the minority always submitting, though sometimes with a very bad grace. Indeed, on one occasion Lanc, who usually differed from the others, threatened to refer the matter to the general vote of the whole crew. There was a constant conflict in the point of view; for whereas Kenna and Hasta were anxious to extend the Saxon power, and to make it greater in the eyes of the world, Lanc was of opinion that they should give less thought to conquest and more to the comfort and advancement of their followers. At the same time it seemed to me that really Lanc was the most combative of the three; so much so that, even in time of peace, he could not forgo this contest with his own brethren. Neither of the others seemed very fond of him, for they were each, as was easy to see, proud of their chieftainship, and anxious to use their authority, referring continually to those noble ancestors from whom it was derived; while Lanc, though he was equally well born, took the view of the common men upon every occasion, claiming that the interests of the many were superior to the privileges of the few. In a word, Crassus, if you could imagine a freebooting Gracchus* on one side, and two piratical patricians upon the other, you would understand the effect which my companions produced upon me.

There was one peculiarity which I observed in their conversation which soothed me very much. I am fond of these Britons, among whom I have spent so much of my life, and I wish them well. It was very pleasing, therefore, to notice that these men insisted upon it in their conversation that the whole object of their visit was the good of the islanders. Any prospect of advantage to themselves was pushed into the background. I was not clear that these professions could be made to agree with the speech in which Kenna had promised a hundred hides of land to every man on the ship; but on my making this remark, the three chiefs seemed very surprised and hurt by my suspicions, and explained very plausibly that, as the Britons needed them as a guard, they could not aid them better than by settling on the soil, and so being continually at hand in order to help them. In time, they said, they hoped to raise and train the natives to such a point that they would be able to look after themselves. Lanc spoke with some degree of eloquence upon the nobleness of the mission which they had undertaken, and the others clattered their cups of mead (a jar of that unpleasant drink was on the table) in token of their agreement.

I observed also how much interested, and how very earnest and intolerant these barbarians were in the matter of religion. Of Christianity they knew nothing, so that although they were aware that the Britons were Christians, they had not a notion of what their creed really was. Yet without examination they started by taking it for granted that their own worship of Woden was absolutely right, and that therefore this other creed must be absolutely wrong. "This vile religion", "this sad superstition" and "this grievous error" were among the phrases which they used towards it. Instead of expressing pity for anyone who had been misinformed upon so serious a question, their feelings were those of anger, and they declared most earnestly that they would spare no pains to set the matter right, fingering the hilts of their long broadswords as they said so.

Well, my dear Crassus, you will have had enough of me and of my Saxons. I have given you a short sketch of these people and their ways. Since I began this letter, I have visited the two other ships which have come in, and as I find the same characteristics among the people on board them, I cannot doubt that they lie deeply in the race. For the rest, they are brave, hardy and very pertinacious in all that they undertake; whereas the Britons, though a great deal more spirited, have not the same steadiness of purpose, their quicker imaginations suggesting always some other course, and their more fiery passions being succeeded by reaction. When I looked from the deck of the first Saxon ship, and saw the swaying excited multitude of Britons on the beach, contrasting them with the intent, silent men who stood beside me, it seemed to me more than ever dangerous to call in such allies. So strongly did I feel it that I turned to Kenna, who was also looking towards the beach.

"You will own this island before you have finished," said I.

His eyes sparkled as he gazed. "Perhaps," he cried; and then suddenly correcting himself and thinking that he had said too much, he added:

"A temporary occupation – nothing more."

An Iconoclast

I T WAS DAYBREAK of a March morning in the year of Christ 92. Outside the long Semita Alta* was already thronged with people, with buyers and sellers, callers and strollers, for the Romans were so early-rising a people that many a patrician preferred to see his clients at six in the morning. Such was the good republican tradition, still upheld by the more conservative; but with more modern habits of luxury, a night of pleasure and banqueting was no uncommon thing. Thus one, who had learnt the new and yet adhered to the old, might find his hours overlap, and without so much as a pretence of sleep come straight from his night of debauch into his day of business, turning with heavy wits and an aching head to that round of formal duties which consumed the life of a Roman gentleman.

So it was with Emilius Flaccus that March morning. He and his fellow senator, Caius Balbus, had passed the night in one of those gloomy drinking bouts to which the Emperor Domitian* summoned his chosen friends at the high palace on the Palatine. Now, having reached the portals of the house of Flaccus, they stood together under the pomegranate-fringed portico which fronted the peristyle and, confident in each other's tried discretion, made up by the freedom of their criticism for the long self-suppression of that melancholy feast.

"If he would but feed his guests," said Balbus, a little red-faced, choleric nobleman with yellow-shot angry eyes. "What had we? Upon my life, I have forgotten. Plovers' eggs, a mess of fish, some bird or other and then his eternal apples."

"Of which," said Flaccus, "he ate only the apples. Do him the justice to confess that he takes even less than he gives. At least they cannot say of him as of Vitellius, that his teeth beggared the empire."*

"No, nor his thirst either, great as it is. That fiery Sabine wine of his could be had for a few sesterces the amphora. It is the common drink of the carters at every wine house on the country roads. I longed for a glass of my own rich Falernian or the mellow Coan that was bottled in the year that Titus took Jerusalem.* Is it even now too late? Could we not wash this rasping stuff from our palates?"

"Nay, better come in with me now and take a bitter draught ere you go upon your way. My Greek physician Stephanos has a rare prescription for a morning head. What! Your clients await you? Well, I will see you later at the Senate house."

The patrician had entered his atrium, bright with rare flowers, and melodious with strange singing birds. At the jaws of the hall, true to his morning duties, stood Lebs, the little Nubian slave, with snow-white tunic and turban, a salver of glasses in one hand, whilst in the other he held a flask of thin lemon-tinted liquid. The master of the house filled up a bitter aromatic bumper, and was about to drink it off, when his hand was arrested by a sudden perception that something was much amiss in his household. It was to be read all around him – in the frightened eyes of the black boy, in the agitated face of the keeper of the atrium, in the gloom and silence of the little knot of *ordinarii*,* the procurator or major-domo at their head, who had assembled to greet their master. Stephanos the physician, Cleios the Alexandrine reader, Promus the steward each turned his head away to avoid his master's questioning gaze.

"What in the name of Pluto is the matter with you all?" cried the amazed senator, whose night of potations had left him in no mood for patience. "Why do you stand moping there? Stephanos, Vacculus, is anything amiss? Here, Promus, you are the head of my household. What is it, then? Why do you turn your eyes away from me?"

The burly steward, whose fat face was haggard and mottled with anxiety, laid his hand upon the sleeve of the domestic beside him.

"Sergius is responsible for the atrium, my lord. It is for him to tell you the terrible thing that has befallen in your absence."

"Nay, it was Datus who did it. Bring him in, and let him explain it himself," said Sergius in a sulky voice.

The patience of the patrician was at an end. "Speak this instant, you rascal!" he shouted angrily. "Another minute, and I will have you dragged to the *ergastulum*,* where, with your feet in the stocks and the gyves round your wrists, you may learn quicker obedience. Speak, I say, and without delay."

"It is the Venus," the man stammered. "The Greek Venus of Praxiteles."*

The senator gave a cry of apprehension and rushed to the corner of the atrium, where a little shrine, curtained off by silken drapery, held the precious statue, the greatest art treasure of his collection – perhaps of the whole world. He tore the hangings aside and stood in speechless anger before the outraged goddess. The red, perfumed lamp which always burned before her had been spilt and broken; her altar fire had been quenched, her chaplet had been dashed aside. But worst of all – insufferable sacrilege! – her own beautiful nude body of glistening Pentelic marble,* as white and fair as when the inspired Greek had hewed it out five hundred years before, had been most brutally mishandled. Three fingers of the gracious outstretched hand had been struck off, and lay upon the pedestal beside her. Above her delicate breast a dark mark showed, where a blow had disfigured the marble.

Emilius Flaccus, the most delicate and judicious connoisseur in Rome, stood gasping and croaking, his hand to his throat, as he gazed at his disfigured masterpiece. Then he turned upon his slaves, his fury in his convulsed face; but, to his amazement, they were not looking at him, but had all turned in attitudes of deep respect towards the opening of the peristyle. As he faced round and saw who had just entered his house, his own rage fell away from him in an instant, and his manner became as humble as that of his servants.

The newcomer was a man forty-three years of age, clean-shaven, with a massive head, large engorged eyes, a small clear-cut nose, and the full bull neck which was the especial mark of his breed. He had entered through the peristyle with a swaggering, rolling gait, as one who walks upon his own ground, and now he stood, his hands upon his hips, looking round him at the bowing slaves, and finally at their master, with a half-humorous expression upon his flushed and brutal face.

"Why, Emilius," said he, "I had understood that your household was the best-ordered in Rome. What is amiss with you this morning?"

"Nothing could be amiss with us now that Caesar has deigned to come under my roof," said the courtier. "This is indeed a most glad surprise which you have prepared for me."

"It was an afterthought," said Domitian. "When you and the others had left me, I was in no mood for sleep, and so it came into my mind that I would have a breath of morning air by coming down to you, and seeing this Grecian Venus of yours, about which you discoursed so eloquently between the cups. But, indeed, by your appearance and that of your servants, I should judge that my visit was an ill-timed one."

"Nay, dear master; say not so. But, indeed, it is truth that I was in trouble at the moment of your welcome entrance, and this trouble was, as the Fates have willed it, brought forth by that very statue in which you have been graciously pleased to show your interest. There it stands, and you can see for yourself how rudely it has been mishandled."

"By Pluto and all the nether gods, if it were mine some of you should feed the lampreys," said the Emperor, looking round with his fierce eyes at the shrinking slaves. "You were always over-merciful, Emilius. It is the common talk that your *catenæ** are rusted for want of use. But surely this is beyond all bounds. Let me see how you handle the matter. Whom do you hold responsible?"

"The slave Sergius is responsible, since it is his place to tend the atrium," said Flaccus. "Stand forward, Sergius. What have you to say?"

The trembling slave advanced to his master. "If it please you, sir, the mischief has been done by Datus the Christian."

"Datus! Who is he?"

"The *matulator*, the scavenger, my lord. I did not know that he belonged to these horrible people, or I should not have admitted him. He came with his broom to brush out the litter of the birds. His eyes fell upon the Venus, and in an instant he had rushed upon her and struck her two blows with his wooden besom. Then we fell upon him and dragged him away. But alas! Alas! It was too late, for already the wretch had dashed off the fingers of the goddess."

The Emperor smiled grimly, while the patrician's thin face grew pale with anger.

"Where is the fellow?" he asked.

"In the *ergastulum*, your honour, with the *furca** on his neck."

"Bring him hither and summon the household."

A few minutes later the whole back of the atrium was thronged by the motley crowd who ministered to the household needs of a great Roman nobleman. There was the *arcarius*, or account keeper, with his stylus behind his ear; the sleek *prægustator*, who sampled all foods, so as to stand between his master and poison, and beside him his predecessor, now a half-witted idiot through the interception twenty years before of a datura* draught from Canidia; the cellar man, summoned from amongst his amphorae; the cook, with his basting ladle in his hand; the pompous *nomenclator*, who ushered the guests; the *cubicularius*, who saw to their accommodation; the *silentiarius*, who kept order in the house; the *structor*, who set forth the tables; the *carptor*, who carved the food; the *cinerarius*, who lit the fires – these and many more, half-curious, half-terrified, came to the judging of Datus. Behind them a chattering, giggling swarm of Lalages, Marias, Cerusas and Amaryllides, from the laundries and the spinning rooms, stood upon their tiptoes, and extended their pretty wondering faces over the shoulders of the men. Through this crowd came two stout varlets leading the culprit between them. He was a small, dark, rough-headed man, with an unkempt beard and wild eyes which shone brightly with strong inward emotion. His hands were bound behind him, and over his neck was the heavy wooden collar or *furca* which was placed upon refractory slaves. A smear of blood across his cheek showed that he had not come uninjured from the preceding scuffle.

"Are you Datus the scavenger?" asked the patrician.

The man drew himself up proudly. "Yes," said he, "I am Datus."

"Did you do this injury to my statue?"

"Yes, I did."

There was an uncompromising boldness in the man's reply which compelled respect. The wrath of his master became tinged with interest.

"Why did you do this?" he asked.

"Because it was my duty."

"Why, then, was it your duty to destroy your master's property?"

"Because I am a Christian." His eyes blazed suddenly out of his dark face. "Because there is no God but the one eternal, and all else are sticks and stones. What has this naked harlot to do with Him to whom the great firmament is but a garment and the earth a footstool? It was in His service that I have broken your statue."

Domitian looked with a smile at the patrician. "You will make nothing of him," said he. "They speak even so when they stand before the lions in the arena. As to argument, not all the philosophers of Rome can break them down. Before my very face they refuse to sacrifice in my honour. Never were such impossible people to deal with. I should take a short way with him if I were you."

"What would Caesar advise?"

"There are the games this afternoon. I am showing the new hunting leopard which King Juba has sent from Numidia. This slave may give us some sport when he finds the hungry beast sniffing at his heels."

The patrician considered for a moment. He had always been a father to his servants. It was hateful to him to think of any injury befalling them. Perhaps even now, if this strange fanatic would show his sorrow for what he had done, it might be possible to spare him. At least it was worth trying.

"Your offence deserves death," he said. "What reasons can you give why it should not befall you, since you have injured this statue, which is worth your own price a hundred times over?"

The slave looked steadfastly at his master. "I do not fear death," he said. "My sister Candida died in the arena, and I am ready to do the same. It is true that I have injured your statue, but I am able to find you something of far greater value in exchange. I will give you the truth and the gospel in exchange for your broken idol."

The Emperor laughed. "You will do nothing with him, Emilius," he said. "I know his breed of old. He is ready to die; he says so himself. Why save him, then?"

But the patrician still hesitated. He would make a last effort.

"Throw off his bonds," he said to the guards. "Now take the *furca* off his neck. So! Now, Datus, I have released you to show you that I trust you. I have no wish to do you any hurt if you will but acknowledge your error, and so set a better example to my household here assembled."

"How then, shall I acknowledge my error?" the slave asked.

"Bow your head before the goddess, and entreat her forgiveness for the violence you have done her. Then perhaps you may gain my pardon as well."

"Put me, then, before her," said the Christian.

Emilius Flaccus looked triumphantly at Domitian. By kindness and tact he was effecting that which the Emperor had failed to do by violence. Datus walked in front of the mutilated Venus. Then with a sudden spring he tore the baton out of the hand of one of his guardians, leapt upon the pedestal, and showered his blows upon the lovely marble woman. With a crack and a dull thud her right arm dropped to the ground. Another fierce blow and the left had followed. Flaccus danced and screamed with horror, while his servants dragged the raving iconoclast from his impassive victim. Domitian's brutal laughter echoed through the hall.

"Well, friend, what think you now?" he cried. "Are you wiser than your Emperor? Can you indeed tame your Christian with kindness?"

Emilius Flaccus wiped the sweat from his brow. "He is yours, great Caesar. Do with him as you will."

"Let him be at the gladiators' entrance of the circus an hour before the games begin," said the Emperor. "Now, Emilius, the night has been a merry one. My Ligurian galley waits by the river quay. Come, cool your head with a spin to Ostia ere the business of state calls you to the Senate."

Giant Maximin

I – THE COMING OF MAXIMIN

MANY ARE THE STRANGE vicissitudes of history. Greatness has often sunk to the dust, and has tempered itself to its new surrounding. Smallness has risen aloft, has flourished for a time, and then has sunk once more. Rich monarchs have become poor monks, brave conquerors have lost their manhood, eunuchs and women have overthrown armies and kingdoms. Surely there is no situation which the mind of man could invent which has not taken shape and been played out upon the world stage. But of all the strange careers and of all the wondrous happenings, stranger than Charles in his monastery, or Justin on his throne, there stands the case of Giant Maximin, what he attained, and how he attained it. Let me tell the sober facts of history, tinged only by that colouring to which the more austere historians could not condescend. It is a record as well as a story.

In the heart of Thrace* some ten miles north of the Rhodope mountains, there is a valley which is named Harpessus, after the stream which runs down it. Through this valley lies the main road from the east to the west, and along the road, returning from an expedition against the Alani,* there marched, upon the fifth day of the month of June in the year 210, a small but compact Roman army. It consisted of three legions – the Jovian, the Cappadocian and the men of Hercules. Ten *turmæ** of Gallic cavalry led the van, whilst the rear was covered by a regiment of Batavian Horse Guards, the immediate attendants of the Emperor Septimius Severus,* who had conducted the campaign in person. The peasants who lined the low hills which fringed the valley looked with indifference upon the long files of dusty, heavily burdened infantry, but they broke into murmurs of delight at the gold-faced cuirasses and high brazen horse-hair helmets of the guardsmen, applauding their stalwart figures, their martial bearing and the stately black chargers which they rode. A soldier might know that it was the little weary men with their short swords, their heavy pikes over their shoulders and their square shields slung upon their backs who were the real terror of the enemies of the empire, but to the eyes of the wondering Thracians it was this troop of glittering Apollos who bore Rome's victory upon their banners, and upheld the throne of the purple-togaed prince who rode before them.

Among the scattered groups of peasants who looked on from a respectful distance at this military pageant, there were two men who attracted much attention from those who stood immediately around them. The one was commonplace enough – a little grey-headed man, with uncouth dress and a frame which was bent and warped by a long life of arduous toil, goat-driving and wood-chopping, among the mountains. It was the appearance of his youthful companion which had drawn the amazed observation of the bystanders. In stature he was such a giant as is seen but once or twice in each generation of mankind. Eight feet and two inches was his measure from his sandalled sole to the topmost curls of his tangled hair. Yet for all his mighty stature there was nothing heavy or clumsy in the man. His huge shoulders bore no redundant flesh, and his figure was straight and hard and supple as a young pine tree. A frayed suit of brown leather clung close to his giant body, and a cloak of undressed sheepskin was slung from his shoulder. His bold blue eyes, shock of yellow hair and fair skin showed that he was of Gothic or northern blood, and the amazed expression upon his broad frank face as he stared at the passing troops told of a simple and uneventful life in some back valley of the Macedonian mountains.

"I fear your mother was right when she advised that we keep you at home," said the old man anxiously. "Tree-cutting and wood-carrying will seem but dull work after such a sight as this."

"When I see mother next it will be to put a golden torque round her neck," said the young giant. "And you, Daddy; I will fill your leather pouch with gold pieces before I have done."

The old man looked at his son with startled eyes. "You would not leave us, Theckla! What could we do without you?"

"My place is down among yonder men," said the young man. "I was not born to drive goats and carry logs, but to sell this manhood of mine in the best market. There is my market in the Emperor's own guard. Say nothing, Daddy, for my mind is set, and if you weep now it will be to laugh hereafter. I will to great Rome with the soldiers."

The daily march of the heavily laden Roman legionary was fixed at twenty miles; but on this afternoon, though only half the distance had been accomplished, the silver trumpets blared out their welcome news that a camp was to be formed. As the men broke their ranks, the reason of their light march was announced by the decurions.* It was the birthday of Geta, the younger son of the Emperor, and in his honour there would be games and a double ration of wine. But the iron discipline of the Roman army required that under all circumstances certain duties should be performed, and foremost among them that the camp should be made secure. Laying down their arms in the order of their ranks, the soldiers seized their spades and axes, and worked rapidly and joyously until sloping vallum and gaping fossa* girdled them round, and gave them safe refuge against a night attack. Then in noisy, laughing, gesticulating crowds they gathered in their thousands round the grassy arena where the sports were to be held. A long green hillside sloped down to a level plain, and on this gentle incline the army lay watching the strife of the chosen athletes who contended before them. They stretched themselves in the glare of the sunshine, their heavy tunics thrown off, and their naked limbs sprawling, wine cups and baskets of fruit and cakes circling amongst them, enjoying rest and peace as only those can to whom it comes so rarely.

The five-mile race was over, and had been won as usual by Decurion Brennus, the crack long-distance champion of the Herculians. Amid the yells of the Jovians, Capellus of the corps had carried off both the long and the high jump. Big Brebix the Gaul had out-thrown the long guardsman Serenus with the fifty-pound stone. Now, as the sun sank towards the western ridge, and turned the Harpessus to a riband of gold, they had come to the final of the wrestling, where the pliant Greek, whose name is lost in the nickname of "Python", was tried out against the bull-necked lictor of the military police, a hairy Hercules, whose heavy hand had in the way of duty oppressed many of the spectators.

As the two men, stripped save for their loincloths, approached the wrestling ring, cheers and counter-cheers burst from their adherents, some favouring the lictor for his Roman blood, some the Greek from their own private grudge. And then, of a sudden, the cheering died, heads were turned towards the slope away from the arena, men stood up and peered and pointed, until finally, in a strange hush, the whole great assembly had forgotten the athletes, and were watching a single man walking swiftly towards them down the green curve of the hill. This huge solitary figure, with the oaken club in his hand, the shaggy fleece flapping from his great shoulders and the setting sun gleaming upon a halo of golden hair, might have been the tutelary god of the fierce and barren mountains from which he had issued. Even the Emperor rose from his chair and gazed with open-eyed amazement at the extraordinary being who approached him.

The man, whom we already know as Theckla the Thracian, paid no heed to the attention which he had aroused, but strode onwards, stepping as lightly as a deer, until he reached the fringe of the soldiers. Amid their open ranks he picked his way, sprang over the ropes which guarded the arena and advanced towards the Emperor, until a spear at his breast warned him that he must go no nearer. Then he sunk upon his right knee and called out some words in the Gothic speech.

"Great Jupiter! Whoever saw such a body of a man!" cried the Emperor. "What says he? What is amiss with the fellow? Whence comes he, and what is his name?"

An interpreter translated the barbarian's answer. "He says, great Caesar, that he is of good blood, and sprung by a Gothic father from a woman of the Alani. He says that his name is Theckla, and that he would fain carry a sword in Caesar's service."

The Emperor smiled. "Some post could surely be found for such a man, were it but as janitor at the Palatine Palace," said he to one of the prefects. "I would fain see him walk even as he is through the forum. He would turn the heads of half the women in Rome. Talk to him, Crassus. You know his speech."

The Roman officer turned to the giant. "Caesar says that you are to come with him, and he will make you the servant at his door."

The barbarian rose, and his fair cheeks flushed with resentment.

"I will serve Caesar as a soldier," said he, "but I will be house servant to no man – not even to him. If Caesar would see what manner of man I am, let him put one of his guardsmen up against me."

"By the shade of Milo this is a bold fellow!" cried the Emperor. "How say you, Crassus? Shall he make good his words?"

"By your leave, Caesar," said the blunt soldier, "good swordsmen are too rare in these days that we should let them slay each other for sport. Perhaps if the barbarian would wrestle a fall—"

"Excellent!" cried the Emperor. "Here is the Python, and here Varus the Lictor, each stripped for the bout. Have a look at them, barbarian, and see which you would choose. What does he say? He would take them both? Nay then he is either the king of wrestlers or the king of boasters, and we shall soon see which. Let him have his way, and he has himself to thank if he comes out with a broken neck."

There was some laughter when the peasant tossed his sheepskin mantle to the ground and, without troubling to remove his leathern tunic, advanced towards the two wrestlers; but it became uproarious when with a quick spring he seized the Greek under one arm and the Roman under the other, holding them as in a vice. Then with a terrific effort he tore them both from the ground, carried them writhing and kicking round the arena, and finally walking up to the Emperor's throne, threw his two athletes down in front of him. Then, bowing to Caesar, the huge barbarian withdrew, and laid his great bulk down among the ranks of the applauding soldiers, whence he watched with stolid unconcern the conclusion of the sports.

It was still daylight when the last event had been decided, and the soldiers returned to the camp. The Emperor Severus had ordered his horse, and in the company of Crassus, his favourite prefect, rode down the winding pathway which skirts the Harpessus, chatting over the future dispersal of the army. They had ridden for some miles when Severus, glancing behind him, was surprised to see a huge figure which trotted lightly along at the very heels of his horse.

"Surely this is Mercury as well as Hercules that we have found among the Thracian mountains," said he with, a smile. "Let us see how soon our Syrian horses can out-distance him." The two Romans broke into a gallop, and did not draw rein until a good mile had been covered at the full pace of their splendid chargers. Then they turned and looked back; but there, some distance off, still running with a lightness and a spring which spoke of iron muscles and inexhaustible endurance, came the great barbarian. The Roman Emperor waited until the athlete had come up to them.

"Why do you follow me?" he asked.

"It is my hope, Caesar, that I may always follow you." His flushed face as he spoke was almost level with that of the mounted Roman.

"By the god of war, I do not know where in all the world I could find such a servant!" cried the Emperor. "You shall be my own bodyguard, the one nearest to me of all."

The giant fell upon his knee. "My life and strength are yours," he said. "I ask no more than to spend them for Caesar."

Crassus had interpreted this short dialogue. He now turned to the Emperor.

"If he is indeed to be always at your call, Caesar, it would be well to give the poor barbarian some name which your lips can frame. Theckla is as uncouth and craggy a word as one of his native rocks."

The Emperor pondered for a moment. "If I am to have the naming of him," said he, "then surely I shall call him Maximus, for there is not such a giant upon earth."

"Hark you," said the prefect. "The Emperor has deigned to give you a Roman name, since you have come into his service. Henceforth you are no longer Theckla, but you are Maximus. Can you say it after me?"

"Maximin," repeated the barbarian, trying to catch the Roman word.

The Emperor laughed at the mincing accent. "Yes, yes, Maximin let it be. To all the world you are Maximin, the bodyguard of Severus. When we have reached Rome, we will soon see that your dress shall correspond with your office. Meanwhile march with the guard until you have my further orders."

So it came about that as the Roman army resumed its march next day, and left behind it the fair valley of the

Harpessus, a huge recruit, clad in brown leather, with a rude sheepskin floating from his shoulders, marched beside the Imperial troop. But far away in the wooden farmhouse of a distant Macedonian valley two old country folk wept salt tears, and prayed to the gods for the safety of their boy who had turned his face to Rome.

II – THE RISE OF GIANT MAXIMIN

EXACTLY TWENTY-FIVE YEARS had passed since the day that Theckla the huge Thracian peasant had turned into Maximin the Roman guardsman. They had not been good years for Rome. Gone for ever were the great Imperial days of the Hadrians and the Trajans. Gone also the golden age of the two Antonines, when the highest were for once the most worthy and most wise. It had been an epoch of weak and cruel men. Severus, the swarthy African, a stark grim man, had died in far away York, after fighting all the winter with the Caledonian Highlanders – a race who have ever since worn the martial garb of the Romans. His son, known only by his slighting nickname of Caracalla, had reigned during six years of insane lust and cruelty, before the knife of an angry soldier avenged the dignity of the Roman name. The nonentity Macrinus had filled the dangerous throne for a single year before he also met a bloody end, and made room for the most grotesque of all monarchs, the unspeakable Heliogabalus with his foul mind and his painted face. He in turn was cut to pieces by the soldiers; and Severus Alexander,* a gentle youth, scarce seventeen years of age, had been thrust into his place. For thirteen years now he had ruled, striving with some success to put some virtue and stability into the rotting empire, but raising many fierce enemies as he did so – enemies whom he had not the strength nor the wit to hold in check.

And Giant Maximin – what of him? He had carried his eight feet of manhood through the lowlands of Scotland and the passes of the Grampians. He had seen Severus pass away, and had soldiered with his son. He had fought in Armenia, in Dacia and in Germany. They had made him a centurion upon the field when with his hands he plucked out one by one the stockades of a northern village, and so cleared a path for the stormers. His strength had been the jest and the admiration of the soldiers. Legends about him had spread through the army, and were the common gossip round the campfires – of his duel with the German axeman on the Island of the Rhine, and of the blow with his fist that broke the leg of a Scythian's horse. Gradually he had won his way upwards, until now, after quarter of a century's service, he was tribune of the fourth legion and superintendent of recruits for the whole army. The young soldier who had come under the glare of Maximin's eyes, or had been lifted up with one huge hand while he was cuffed by the other, had his first lesson from him in the discipline of the service.

It was nightfall in the camp of the fourth legion upon the Gallic shore of the Rhine. Across the moonlit water, amid the thick forests which stretched away to the dim horizon, lay the wild untamed German tribes. Down on the riverbank the light gleamed upon the helmets of the Roman sentinels who kept guard along the river. Far away a red point rose and fell in the darkness – a watchfire of the enemy upon the farther shore.

Outside his tent, beside some smouldering logs, Giant Maximin was seated, a dozen of his officers around him. He had changed much since the day when we first met him in the valley of the Harpessus. His huge frame was as erect as ever, and there was no sign of diminution of his strength. But he had aged nonetheless. The yellow tangle of hair was gone, worn down by the ever-pressing helmet. The fresh young face was drawn and hardened, with austere lines wrought by trouble and privation. The nose was more hawk-like, the eyes more cunning, the expression more cynical and more sinister. In his youth, a child would have run to his arms. Now it would shrink screaming from his gaze. That was what twenty-five years with the eagles had done for Theckla the Thracian peasant.

He was listening now – for he was a man of few words – to the chatter of his centurions. One of them, Balbus the Sicilian, had been to the main camp at Mainz, only four miles away, and had seen the Emperor Alexander arrive that very day from Rome. The rest were eager at the news, for it was a time of unrest, and the rumour of great changes was in the air.

"How many had he with him?" asked Labienus, a black-browed veteran from the south of Gaul. "I'll wager a month's pay that he was not so trustful as to come alone among his faithful legions."

"He had no great force," replied Balbus. "Ten or twelve cohorts of the praetorians and a handful of horse."

"Then indeed his head is in the lion's mouth," cried Sulpicius, a hot-headed youth from the African Pentapolis.* "How was he received?"

"Coldly enough. There was scarce a shout as he came down the line."

"They are ripe for mischief," said Labienus. "And who can wonder, when it is we soldiers who uphold the empire upon our spears, while the lazy citizens at Rome reap all of our sowing? Why cannot a soldier have what the soldier gains? So long as they throw us our denarius a day, they think that they have done with us."

"Aye," croaked a grumbling old greybeard. "Our limbs, our blood, our lives – what do they care so long as the barbarians are held off, and they are left in peace to their feastings and their circus? Free bread, free wine, free games – everything for the loafer at Rome. For us the frontier guard and a soldier's fare."

Maximin gave a deep laugh. "Old Plancus talks like that," said he, "but we know that for all the world he would not change his steel plate for a citizen's gown. You've earned the kennel, old hound, if you wish it. Go and gnaw your bone and growl in peace."

"Nay, I am too old for change. I will follow the eagle till I die. And yet I had rather die in serving a soldier master than a long-gowned Syrian who comes of a stock where the women are men and the men are women."

There was a laugh from the circle of soldiers, for sedition and mutiny were rife in the camp, and even the old centurion's outbreak could not draw a protest. Maximin raised his great mastiff head and looked at Balbus.

"Was any name in the mouths of the soldiers?" he asked in a meaning voice.

There was a hush for the answer. The sigh of the wind among the pines and the low lapping of the river swelled out louder in the silence. Balbus looked hard at his commander.

"Two names were whispered from rank to rank," said he. "One was Ascenius Pollio, the general. The other was—"

The fiery Sulpicius sprang to his feet waving a glowing brand above his head.

"Maximinus!" he yelled. "Imperator Maximinus Augustus!"

Who could tell how it came about? No one had thought of it an hour before. And now it sprang in an instant to full accomplishment. The shout of the frenzied young African had scarcely rung through the darkness when from the tents, from the watchfires, from the sentries, the answer came pealing back: "Ave Maximinus! Ave Maximinus Augustus!" From all sides men came rushing, half-clad, wild-eyed, their eyes staring, their mouths agape, flaming wisps of straw or flaring torches above their heads. The giant was caught up by scores of hands, and sat enthroned upon the bull necks of the legionaries. "To the camp!" they yelled. "To the camp! Hail! Hail to the soldier Caesar!"

That same night Severus Alexander, the young Syrian Emperor, walked outside his praetorian camp, accompanied by his friend Licinius Probus, the captain of the guard. They were talking gravely of the gloomy faces and seditious bearing of the soldiers. A great foreboding of evil weighed heavily upon the Emperor's heart, and it was reflected upon the stern bearded face of his companion.

"I like it not," said he. "It is my counsel, Caesar, that with the first light of morning we make our way south once more."

"But surely," the Emperor answered, "I could not for shame turn my back upon the danger. What have they against me? How have I harmed them that they should forget their vows and rise upon me?"

"They are like children who ask always for something new. You heard the murmur as you rode along the ranks. Nay, Caesar, fly tomorrow, and your praetorians will see that you are not pursued. There may be some loyal cohorts among the legions, and if we join forces—"

A distant shout broke in upon their conversation – a low continued roar, like the swelling tumult of a sweeping wave. Far down the road upon which they stood there twinkled many moving lights, tossing and sinking as they rapidly advanced, whilst the hoarse tumultuous bellowing broke into articulate words, the same tremendous words, a thousand-fold repeated. Licinius seized the Emperor by the wrist and dragged him under the cover of some bushes.

"Be still, Caesar! For your life be still!" he whispered. "One word and we are lost!"

Crouching in the darkness, they saw that wild procession pass, the rushing, screaming figures, the tossing arms, the bearded, distorted faces, now scarlet and now grey, as the brandished torches waxed or waned. They heard the rush of many feet, the clamour of hoarse voices, the clang of metal upon metal. And then suddenly, above them all, they saw a vision of a monstrous man, a huge bowed back, a savage face, grim hawk eyes, that looked out over the swaying shields. It was seen for an instant in a smoke-fringed circle of fire, and then it had swept on into the night.

"Who is he?" stammered the Emperor, clutching at his guardsman's sleeve. "They call him Caesar."

"It is surely Maximin the Thracian peasant." In the darkness the praetorian officer looked with strange eyes at his master.

"It is all over, Caesar. Let us fly together to your tent."

But even as they went a second shout had broken forth tenfold louder than the first. If the one had been the roar of the oncoming wave, the other was the full turmoil of the tempest. Twenty thousand voices from the camp had broken into one wild shout which echoed through the night, until the distant Germans round their watchfires listened in wonder and alarm.

"Ave!" cried the voices. "Ave Maximinus Augustus!"

High upon their bucklers stood the giant, and looked round him at the great floor of upturned faces below. His own savage soul was stirred by the clamour, but only his gleaming eyes spoke of the fire within. He waved his hand to the shouting soldiers as the huntsman waves to the leaping pack. They passed him up a coronet of oak leaves, and clashed their swords in homage as he placed it on his head. And then there came a swirl in the crowd before him, a little space was cleared, and there knelt an officer in the praetorian garb, blood upon his face, blood upon his baréd forearm, blood upon his naked sword. Licinius too had gone with the tide.

"Hail, Caesar, hail!" he cried, as he bowed his head before the giant. "I come from Alexander. He will trouble you no more."

III – THE FALL OF MAXIMIN

FOR THREE YEARS the soldier Emperor* had been upon the throne. His palace had been his tent, and his people had been the legionaries. With them he was supreme; away from them he was nothing. He had gone with them from one frontier to the other. He had fought against Dacians, Sarmatians and once again against the Germans. But Rome knew nothing of him, and all her turbulence rose against a master who cared so little for her or her opinion that he never deigned to set foot within her walls. There were cabals and conspiracies against the absent Caesar. Then his heavy hand fell upon them, and they were cuffed, even as the young soldiers had been who passed under his discipline. He knew nothing, and cared as much for consuls, senates and civil laws. His own will and the power of the sword were the only forces which he could understand. Of commerce and the arts he was as ignorant as when he left his Thracian home. The whole vast empire was to him a huge machine for producing the money by which the legions were to be rewarded. Should he fail to get that money, his fellow soldiers would bear him a grudge. To watch their interests they had raised him upon their shields that night. If city funds had to be plundered or temples desecrated, still the money must be got. Such was the point of view of Giant Maximin.

But there came resistance, and all the fierce energy of the man, all the hardness which had given him the leadership of hard men, sprang forth to quell it. From his youth he had lived amidst slaughter. Life and death were cheap things to him. He struck savagely at all who stood up to him, and when they hit back, he struck more savagely still. His giant shadow lay black across the empire from Britain to Syria. A strange subtle vindictiveness became also apparent in him. Omnipotence ripened every fault and swelled it into crime. In the old days he had been rebuked for his roughness. Now a sullen, dangerous anger rose against those who had rebuked him. He sat by the hour with his craggy chin between his hands, and his elbows resting on his knees, while he recalled all the misadventures, all the vexations of his early youth, when Roman wits had shot their little satires upon his bulk and his ignorance. He could not write, but his son Verus placed the names upon his tablets, and they were sent to the Governor of Rome. Men who had long forgotten their offence were called suddenly to make most bloody reparation.

A rebellion broke out in Africa, but was quelled by his lieutenant. But the mere rumour of it set Rome in a turmoil. The Senate found something of its ancient spirit. So did the Italian people. They would not be for ever bullied by the legions. As Maximin approached from the frontier, with the sack of rebellious Rome in his mind, he was faced with every sign of a national resistance. The countryside was deserted, the farms abandoned, the fields cleared of crops and cattle. Before him lay the walled town of Aquileia. He flung himself fiercely upon it, but was met by as fierce a resistance. The walls could not be forced, and yet there was no food in the country round for his legions. The men were starving and dissatisfied. What did it matter to them who was emperor? Maximin was no better than themselves. Why should they call down the curse of the whole empire upon their heads by upholding him? He saw their sullen faces and their averted eyes, and he knew that the end had come.

That night he sat with his son Verus in his tent, and he spoke softly and gently as the youth had never heard him speak before. He had spoken thus in old days with Paullina, the boy's mother; but she had been dead these many years, and all that was soft and gentle in the big man had passed away with her. Now her spirit seemed very near him, and his own was tempered by its presence.

"I would have you go back to the Thracian mountains," he said. "I have tried both, boy, and I can tell you that there is no pleasure which power can bring which can equal the breath of the wind and the smell of the kine upon a summer morning. Against you they have no quarrel. Why should they mishandle you? Keep far from Rome and the Romans. Old Eudoxus has money, and to spare. He awaits you with two horses outside the camp. Make for the valley of the Harpessus, lad. It was thence that your father came, and there you will find his kin. Buy and stock a homestead, and keep yourself far from the paths of greatness and of danger. God keep you, Verus, and send you safe to Thrace."

When his son had kissed his hand and had left him, the Emperor drew his robe around him and sat long in thought. In his slow brain he revolved the past – his early peaceful days, his years with Severus, his memories of Britain, his long campaigns, his strivings and battlings, all leading to that mad night by the Rhine. His fellow soldiers had loved him then. And now he had read death in their eyes. How had he failed them? Others he might have wronged, but they at least had no complaint against him. If he had his time again, he would think less of them and more of his people, he would try to win love instead of fear, he would live for peace and not for war. If he had his time again! But there were shuffling steps, furtive whispers, and the low rattle of arms outside his tent. A bearded face looked in at him, a swarthy African face that he knew well. He laughed, and baring his arm, he took his sword from the table beside him.

"It is you, Sulpicius," said he. "You have not come to cry 'Ave Imperator Maximin!' as once by the campfire. You are tired of me, and by the gods I am tired of you, and glad to be at the end of it. Come and have done with it, for I am minded to see how many of you I can take with me when I go."

They clustered at the door of the tent, peeping over each other's shoulders, and none wishing to be the first to close with that laughing, mocking giant. But something was pushed forward upon a spear point, and as he saw it, Maximin groaned and his sword sank to the earth.

"You might have spared the boy," he sobbed. "He would not have hurt you. Have done with it then, for I will gladly follow him."

So they closed upon him and cut and stabbed and thrust, until his knees gave way beneath him and he dropped upon the floor.

"The tyrant is dead!" they cried. "The tyrant is dead," and from all the camp beneath them and from the walls of the beleaguered city the joyous cry came echoing back, "He is dead, Maximin is dead!"

I sit in my study, and upon the table before me lies a denarius of Maximin, as fresh as when the triumvir of the Temple of Juno Moneta sent it from the mint. Around it are recorded his resounding titles – Imperator Maximinus, Pontifex Maximus, Tribunitia Potestate, and the rest. In the centre is the impress of a great craggy head, a massive jaw, a rude fighting face, a contracted forehead. For all the pompous roll of titles it is a peasant's face, and I see him not as the Emperor of Rome, but as the great Thracian boor who strode down the hillside on that far-distant summer day when first the eagles beckoned him to Rome.

The Red Star

T HE HOUSE OF THEODOSIUS, the famous eastern merchant, was in the best part of Constantinople at the Sea Point which is near the church of St Demetrius. Here he would entertain in so princely a fashion that even the Emperor Maurice* had been known to come privately from the neighbouring Bucoleon Palace in order to join in the revelry. On the night in question, however, which was the 4th of November in the year of Our Lord 630, his numerous guests had retired early, and there remained only two intimates, both of them successful merchants like himself, who sat with him over their wine on the marble veranda of his house, whence on the one side they could see the lights of the shipping in the Sea of Marmora, and on the other the beacons which marked out the course of the Bosphorus. Immediately at their feet lay a narrow strait of water, with the low, dark loom of the Asiatic hills beyond. A thin haze hid the heavens, but away to the south a single great red star burned sullenly in the darkness.

The night was cool, the light was soothing, and the three men talked freely, letting their minds drift back into the earlier days when they had staked their capital, and often their lives, on the ventures which had built up their present fortunes. The host spoke of his long journeys in North Africa, the land of the Moors; how he had travelled, keeping the blue sea ever upon his right, until he had passed the ruins of Carthage, and so on and ever on until a great tidal ocean beat upon a yellow strand before him, while on the right he could see the high rock across the waves which marked the Pillars of Hercules.* His talk was of dark-skinned, bearded men, of lions and of monstrous serpents. Then Demetrius, the Cilician, an austere man of sixty, told how he also had built up his mighty wealth. He spoke of a journey over the Danube and through the country of the fierce Huns, until he and his friends had found themselves in the mighty forest of Germany, on the shores of the great river which is called the Elbe. His stories were of huge men, sluggish of mind, but murderous in their cups, of sudden midnight broils and nocturnal flights, of villages buried in dense woods, of bloody heathen sacrifices, and of the bears and wolves who haunted the forest paths. So the two elder men capped each other's stories and awoke each other's memories, while Manuel Ducas, the young merchant of gold and ostrich feathers, whose name was already known all over the Levant, sat in silence and listened to their talk. At last, however, they called upon him also for an anecdote, and, leaning his cheek upon his elbow, with his eyes fixed upon the great red star which burned in the south, the younger man began to speak.

"It is the sight of that star which brings a story into my mind," said he. "I do not know its name. Old Lascaris the astronomer would tell me if I asked, but I have no desire to know. Yet at this time of the year I always look out for it, and I never fail to see it burning in the same place. But it seems to me that it is redder and larger than it was.

"It was some ten years ago that I made an expedition into Abyssinia, where I traded to such good effect that I set forth on my return with more than a hundred camel-loads of skins, ivory, gold, spices and other African produce. I brought them to the sea coast at Arsinoe, and carried them up the Arabian Gulf in five of the small boats of the country. Finally, I landed near Sava, which is a starting point for caravans, and, having assembled my camels and hired a guard of forty men from the wandering Arabs, I set forth for Macoraba.* From this point, which is the sacred city of the idolaters of those parts, one can always join the large caravans which go north twice a year to Jerusalem and the sea coast of Syria.

"Our route was a long and weary one. On our left hand was the Arabian Gulf, lying like a pool of molten metal under the glare of day, but changing to blood-red as the sun sank each evening behind the distant African coast. On our right was a monstrous desert which extends, so far as I know, across the whole of Arabia and away to the distant kingdom of the Persians. For many days we saw no sign of life save our own long, straggling line of laden camels with their tattered, swarthy guardians. In these deserts the soft sand deadens the footfall of the animals, so that their silent progress day after day through a scene which never changes, and which is itself noiseless, becomes at last like a strange dream. Often as I rode behind my caravan, and gazed at the grotesque figures which bore my wares in front of me, I found it hard to believe that it was indeed reality, and that it was I, I, Manuel Ducas, who lived near the Theodosian Gate of Constantinople, and shouted for the Green at the hippodrome* every Sunday afternoon, who was there in so strange a land and with such singular comrades.

"Now and then, far out at sea, we caught sight of the white triangular sails of the boats which these people use, but as they are all pirates, we were very glad to be safely upon shore. Once or twice, too, by the water's edge we saw dwarfish creatures – one could scarcely say if they were men or monkeys – who burrow for homes among the seaweed, drink the pools of brackish water and eat what they can catch. These are the fish-eaters, the Ichthyophagi, of whom old Herodotus talks – surely the lowest of all the human

race. Our Arabs shrank from them with horror, for it is
well known that, should you die in the desert, these little
people will settle on you like carrion crows, and leave not
a bone unpicked. They gibbered and croaked and waved
their skinny arms at us as we passed, knowing well that
they could swim far out to sea if we attempted to pursue
them; for it is said that even the sharks turn with disgust
from their foul bodies.

"We had travelled in this way for ten days, camping every
evening at the vile wells which offered a small quantity of
abominable water. It was our habit to rise very early and to
travel very late, but to halt during the intolerable heat of the
afternoon, when, for want of trees, we would crouch in the
shadow of a sandhill, or, if that were wanting, behind our
own camels and merchandise, in order to escape from the
insufferable glare of the sun. On the seventh day we were
near the point where one leaves the coast in order to strike
inland to Macoraba. We had concluded our midday halt, and
were just starting once more, the sun still being so hot that
we could hardly bear it, when, looking up, I saw a remarkable sight. Standing on a hillock to our right there was a man
about forty feet high, holding in his hand a spear which was
the size of the mast of a large ship. You look surprised, my
friends, and you can therefore imagine my feelings when I
saw such a sight. But my reason soon told me that the object

in front of me was really a wandering Arab, whose form had been enormously magnified by the strange distorting effects which the hot air of the desert is able to cause.

"However, the actual apparition caused more alarm to my companions than the imagined one had to me, for with a howl of dismay they shrank together into a frightened group, all pointing and gesticulating as they gazed at the distant figure. I then observed that the man was not alone, but that from all the sandhills a line of turbaned heads was gazing down upon us. The chief of the escort came running to me, and informed me of the cause of their terror, which was that they recognized, by some peculiarity in their headgear, that these men belonged to the tribe of the Dilwas, the most ferocious and unscrupulous of the Bedouin, who had evidently laid an ambuscade for us at this point with the intention of seizing our caravan. When I thought of all my efforts in Abyssinia, of the length of my journey and of the dangers and fatigues which I had endured, I could not bear to think of this total disaster coming upon me at the last instant and robbing me not only of my profits, but also of my original outlay. It was evident, however, that the robbers were too numerous for us to attempt to defend ourselves, and that we should be very fortunate if we escaped with our lives. Sitting upon a packet, therefore, I commended my soul to our blessed St

Helena, while I watched with despairing eyes the stealthy and menacing approach of the Arab robbers.

"It may have been our own good fortune, or it may have been the handsome offering of beeswax candles – four to the pound – which I had mentally vowed to the blessed Helena, but at that instant I heard a great outcry of joy from among my own followers. Standing up on the packet that I might have a better view, I was overjoyed to see a long caravan – five hundred camels at least – with a numerous armed guard, coming along the route from Macoraba. It is, I need not tell you, the custom of all caravans to combine their forces against the robbers of the desert, and with the aid of these newcomers we had become the stronger party. The marauders recognized it at once, for they vanished as if their native sands had swallowed them. Running up to the summit of a sandhill, I was just able to catch a glimpse of a dust cloud whirling away across the yellow plain, with the long necks of their camels, the flutter of their loose garments and the gleam of their spears breaking out from the heart of it. So vanished the marauders.

"Presently I found, however, that I had only exchanged one danger for another. At first I had hoped that this new caravan might belong to some Roman citizen, or at least to some Syrian Christian, but I found that it was entirely Arab. The trading Arabs who are settled in the numerous towns of

Arabia are, of course, very much more peaceable than the Bedouin of the wilderness, those sons of Ishmael of whom we read in Holy Writ. But the Arab blood is covetous and lawless, so that when I saw several hundred of them formed in a semicircle round our camels, looking with greedy eyes at my boxes of precious metals and my packets of ostrich feathers, I feared the worst.

"The leader of the new caravan was a man of dignified bearing and remarkable appearance. His age I would judge to be about forty. He had aquiline features, a noble black beard, and eyes so luminous, so searching and so intense that I cannot remember in all my wanderings to have seen any which could be compared with them. To my thanks and salutations he returned a formal bow, and stood stroking his beard and looking in silence at the wealth which had suddenly fallen into his power. A murmur from his followers showed the eagerness with which they awaited the order to fall upon the plunder, and a young ruffian, who seemed to be on intimate terms with the leader, came to his elbow and put the desires of his companions into words.

"'Surely, oh Revered One,' said he, 'these people and their treasure have been delivered into our hands. When we return with it to the holy place, who of all the Koraish* will fail to see the finger of God which has led us?'

"But the leader shook his head. 'Nay, Ali, it may not be,' he answered. 'This man is, as I judge, a citizen of Rome, and we may not treat him as though he were an idolater.'

"'But he is an unbeliever,' cried the youth, fingering a great knife which hung in his belt. 'Were I to be the judge, he would lose not only his merchandise, but his life also, if he did not accept the faith.'

"The older man smiled and shook his head. 'Nay, Ali, you are too hot-headed,' said he, 'seeing that there are not as yet three hundred faithful in the world, our hands would indeed be full if we were to take the lives and property of all who are not with us. Forget not, dear lad, that charity and honesty are the very nose ring and halter of the true faith.'

"'Among the faithful,' said the ferocious youth.

"'Nay, towards everyone. It is the law of Allah. And yet' – here his countenance darkened, and his eyes shone with a most sinister light – 'the day may soon come when the hour of grace is past, and woe, then, to those who have not hearkened! Then shall the sword of Allah be drawn, and it shall not be sheathed until the harvest is reaped. First it shall strike the idolaters on the day when my own people and kinsmen, the unbelieving Koraish, shall be scattered, and the 360 idols of the Caaba* thrust out upon the dungheaps of the town. Then shall the Caaba be the home and temple of one God only who brooks no rival on earth or in heaven.'

"The man's followers had gathered round him, their spears in their hands, their ardent eyes fixed upon his face, and their dark features convulsed with such fanatic enthusiasm as showed the hold which he had upon their love and respect.

"'We shall be patient,' said he, 'but some time next year, the year after, the day may come when the great angel Gabriel shall bear me the message that the time of words has gone by, and that the hour of the sword has come. We are few and weak, but if it is His will, who can stand against us? Are you of Jewish faith, stranger?' he asked.

"I answered that I was not.

"'The better for you,' he answered, with the same furious anger in his swarthy face. 'First shall the idolaters fall, and then the Jews, in that they have not known those very prophets whom they had themselves foretold. Then last will come the turn of the Christians, who follow indeed a true prophet, greater than Moses or Abraham, but who have sinned in that they have confounded a creature with the Creator. To each in turn – idolater, Jew and Christian – the day of reckoning will come.'

"The ragamuffins behind him all shook their spears as he spoke. There was no doubt about their earnestness, but when I looked at their tattered dresses and simple arms, I could not help smiling to think of their ambitious threats, and to picture what their fate would be upon the day of battle before the battleaxes of our Imperial Guards, or the spears of the heavy cavalry of the Armenian themes.* However, I need not say that I was discreet enough to keep my thoughts to myself, as I had no desire to be the first martyr in this fresh attack upon our blessed faith.

"It was now evening, and it was decided that the two caravans should camp together – an arrangement which was the more welcome as we were by no means sure that we had seen the last of the marauders. I had invited the leader of the Arabs to have supper with me, and after a long exercise of prayer with his followers, he came to join me, but my attempt at hospitality was thrown away, for he would not touch the excellent wine which I had unpacked for him, nor would he eat any of my dainties, contenting himself with stale bread, dried dates and water. After this meal we sat alone by the smouldering fire, the magnificent arch of the heavens above us of that deep, rich blue with those gleaming, clear-cut stars which can only be seen in that dry desert air. Our camp lay before us, and no sound reached our ears save the dull murmur of the voices of our companions and the occasional shrill cry of a jackal among the sandhills around us. Face to face I sat with this strange man, the glow of the fire beating upon his eager and imperious features and reflecting from his passionate eyes. It was the strangest vigil, and one which will never pass from my recollection. I have spoken with many wise and famous men upon my travels, but never with one who left the impression of this one.

"And yet much of his talk was unintelligible to me, though, as you are aware, I speak Arabian like an Arab. It rose and fell in the strangest way. Sometimes it was the babble of a child, sometimes the incoherent raving of a fanatic, sometimes the lofty dreams of a prophet and philosopher. There were times when his stories of demons, of miracles, of dreams and of omens were such as an old woman might tell to please the children of an evening. There were others when, as he talked with shining face of his converse with angels, of the intentions of the Creator and the end of the universe, I felt as if I were in the company of someone more than mortal, someone who was indeed the direct messenger of the Most High.

"There were good reasons why he should treat me with such confidence. He saw in me a messenger to Constantinople and to the Roman Empire. Even as St Paul had brought Christianity to Europe, so he hoped that I might carry his doctrines to my native city. Alas! be the doctrines what they may, I fear that I am not the stuff of which Pauls are made. Yet he strove with all his heart during that long Arabian night to bring me over to his belief. He had with him a holy book, written, as he said, from the dictation of an angel, which he carried in tablets of bone in the nosebag of a camel. Some chapters of this he read me; but, though the precepts were usually good, the language seemed wild and fanciful. There were times when I could scarce keep my countenance as I listened to him. He planned out his future movements, and indeed, as he spoke, it was hard to remember that he was only the wandering leader of an Arab caravan, and not one of the great ones of the earth.

"'When God has given me sufficient power, which will be within a few years,' said he, 'I will unite all Arabia under my banner. Then I will spread my doctrine over Syria and Egypt. When this has been done, I will turn to Persia, and give them the choice of the true faith or the sword. Having taken Persia, it will be easy then to overrun Asia Minor, and so to make our way to Constantinople.'

"I bit my lip to keep from laughing. 'And how long will it be before your victorious troops have reached the Bosphorus?' I asked.

"'Such things are in the hands of God, whose servants we are,' said he. 'It may be that I shall myself have passed away before these things are accomplished, but before the days of our children are completed, all that I have now told you will come to pass. Look at that star,' he added, pointing to a beautiful clear planet above our heads. 'That is the symbol of Christ. See how serene and peaceful it shines, like His own teaching and the memory of His life. Now,' he added, turning his outstretched hand to a dusky red star upon the horizon – the very one on which we are gazing now – 'that is my star, which tells of wrath, of war, of a scourge upon sinners. And yet both are indeed stars, and each does as Allah may ordain.'

"Well, that was the experience which was called to my mind by the sight of this star tonight. Red and angry, it still broods over the south, even as I saw it that night in the desert. Somewhere down yonder that man is working and striving. He may be stabbed by some brother fanatic or slain in a tribal skirmish. If so, that is the end. But if he lives, there was that in his eyes and in his presence which tells me that Mahomet the son of Abdullah – for that was his name – will testify in some noteworthy fashion to the faith that is in him."

The Silver Mirror

3 RD JAN. – This affair of White and Wotherspoon's accounts proves to be a gigantic task. There are twenty thick ledgers to be examined and checked. Who would be a junior partner? However, it is the first big bit of business which has been left entirely in my hands. I must justify it. But it has to be finished so that the lawyers may have the result in time for the trial. Johnson said this morning that I should have to get the last figure out before the 20th of the month. Good Lord! Well, have at it, and if human brain and nerve can stand the strain, I'll win out at the other side. It means office work from ten to five, and then a second sitting from about eight to one in the morning. There's drama in an accountant's life. When I find myself in the still early hours, while all the world sleeps, hunting through column after column for those missing figures which will turn a respected alderman into a felon, I understand that it is not such a prosaic profession after all.

On Monday I came on the first trace of defalcation. No heavy game hunter ever got a finer thrill when first he caught sight of the trail of his quarry. But I look at the twenty ledgers and think of the jungle through which I have to follow him before I get my kill. Hard work – but rare sport, too, in a way! I saw the fat fellow once at a City dinner, his red face glowing above a white napkin. He looked at the little pale man at the end of the table. He would have been pale too if he could have seen the task that would be mine.

6th Jan. – What perfect nonsense it is for doctors to prescribe rest when rest is out of the question! Asses! They might as well shout to a man who has a pack of wolves at his heels that what he wants is absolute quiet. My figures must be out by a certain date; unless they are so, I shall lose the chance of my lifetime, so how on earth am I to rest? I'll take a week or so after the trial.

Perhaps I was myself a fool to go to the doctor at all. But I get nervous and highly strung when I sit alone at my work at night. It's not a pain – only a sort of fullness of the head with an occasional mist over the eyes. I thought perhaps some bromide, or chloral, or something of the kind might do me good. But stop work? It's absurd to ask such a thing. It's like a long-distance race. You feel queer at first and your heart thumps and your lungs pant, but if you have only the pluck to keep on, you get your second wind. I'll stick to my work and wait for my second wind. If it never comes – all the same, I'll stick to my work. Two ledgers are done, and

I am well on in the third. The rascal has covered his tracks well, but I pick them up for all that.

9th Jan. – I had not meant to go to the doctor again. And yet I have had to. "Straining my nerves, risking a complete breakdown, even endangering my sanity." That's a nice sentence to have fired off at one. Well, I'll stand the strain and I'll take the risk, and so long as I can sit in my chair and move a pen I'll follow the old sinner's slot.

By the way, I may as well set down here the queer experience which drove me this second time to the doctor. I'll keep an exact record of my symptoms and sensations, because they are interesting in themselves – "a curious psycho-physiological study," says the doctor – and also because I am perfectly certain that when I am through with them they will all seem blurred and unreal, like some queer dream betwixt sleeping and waking. So now, while they are fresh, I will just make a note of them, if only as a change of thought after the endless figures.

There's an old silver-framed mirror in my room. It was given me by a friend who had a taste for antiquities, and he, as I happen to know, picked it up at a sale and had no notion where it came from. It's a large thing – three feet across and two feet high – and it leans at the back of a side table on my left as I write. The frame is flat, about three inches across, and very old; far too old for hallmarks or other methods of determining its age. The glass part projects, with a bevelled edge, and has the magnificent reflecting power which is only, as it seems to me, to be found in very old mirrors. There's a feeling of perspective when you look into it such as no modern glass can ever give.

The mirror is so situated that as I sit at the table I can usually see nothing in it but the reflection of the red window curtains. But a queer thing happened last night. I had been working for some hours, very much against the grain, with continual bouts of that mistiness of which I had complained. Again and again I had to stop and clear my eyes. Well, on one of these occasions I chanced to look at the mirror. It had the oddest appearance. The red curtains which should have been reflected in it were no longer there, but the glass seemed to be clouded and steamy, not on the surface, which glittered like steel, but deep down in the very grain of it. This opacity, when I stared hard at it, appeared to slowly rotate this way and that, until it was a thick white cloud swirling in heavy wreaths. So real and solid was it, and so reasonable was I, that I remember turning, with the idea that the curtains were on fire. But everything was deadly still in the room – no sound save the ticking of the clock, no movement save the slow gyration of that strange woolly cloud deep in the heart of the old mirror.

Then, as I looked, the mist, or smoke, or cloud, or what-ever one may call it, seemed to coalesce and solidify at two points quite close together, and I was aware, with a thrill of interest rather than of fear, that these were two eyes look-ing out into the room. A vague outline of a head I could see – a woman's by the hair, but this was very shadowy. Only the eyes were quite distinct; such eyes – dark, lumi-nous, filled with some passionate emotion, fury or horror, I could not say which. Never have I seen eyes which were so full of intense, vivid life. They were not fixed upon me, but stared out into the room. Then as I sat erect, passed my hand over my brow, and made a strong conscious effort to pull myself together, the dim head faded into the general opacity, the mirror slowly cleared, and there were the red curtains once again.

A sceptic would say, no doubt, that I had dropped asleep over my figures, and that my experience was a dream. As a matter of fact, I was never more vividly awake in my life. I was able to argue about it even as I looked at it, and to tell myself that it was a subjective impression – a chimera of the nerves – begotten by worry and insomnia. But why this particular shape? And who is the woman, and what is the dreadful emotion which I read in those wonderful brown eyes? They come between me and my work. For the first time I have done less than the daily tally which I had marked out. Perhaps that is why I have had no abnormal sensations tonight. Tomorrow I must wake up, come what may.

11th Jan. – All well, and good progress with my work. I wind the net, coil after coil, round that bulky body. But the last smile may remain with him if my own nerves break over it. The mirror would seem to be a sort of barometer which marks my brain pressure. Each night I have observed that it had clouded before I reached the end of my task.

Dr Sinclair (who is, it seems, a bit of a psychologist) was so interested in my account that he came round this evening to have a look at the mirror. I had observed that something was scribbled in crabbed old characters upon the metalwork at the back. He examined this with a lens, but could make nothing of it. "Sanc. X. Pal." was his final reading of it, but that did not bring us any further. He advised me to put it away into another room; but, after all, whatever I may see in it is, by his own account, only a symptom. It is in the cause that the danger lies. The twenty ledgers – not the silver mirror – should be packed away if I could only do it. I'm at the eighth now, so I progress.

13th Jan. – Perhaps it would have been wiser after all if I had packed away the mirror. I had an extraordinary experience with it last night. And yet I find it so interesting, so fascinating, that even now I will keep it in its place. What on earth is the meaning of it all?

I suppose it was about one in the morning, and I was closing my books preparatory to staggering off to bed, when I saw her there in front of me. The stage of mistiness and development must have passed unobserved, and there she was in all her beauty and passion and distress, as clear-cut as if she were really in the flesh before me. The figure was small, but very distinct – so much so that every feature, and every detail of dress, are stamped in my memory. She is seated on the extreme left of the mirror. A sort of shadowy figure crouches down beside her – I can dimly discern that it is a man – and then behind them is cloud, in which I see figures – figures which move. It is not a mere picture upon which I look. It is a scene in life, an actual episode. She crouches and quivers. The man beside her cowers down. The vague figures make abrupt movements and gestures. All my fears were swallowed up in my interest. It was maddening to see so much and not to see more.

But I can at least describe the woman to the smallest point. She is very beautiful and quite young – not more than five-and-twenty, I should judge. Her hair is of a very rich brown, with a warm chestnut shade fining into gold at the edges. A little flat-pointed cap comes to an angle in front and is made of lace edged with pearls. The forehead is high, too high perhaps for perfect beauty; but one would not have it otherwise, as it gives a touch of power and strength to what would otherwise be a softly feminine face. The brows are most delicately curved over heavy eyelids, and then come those wonderful eyes – so large, so dark, so full of overmastering emotion, of rage and horror, contending with a pride of self-control which holds her from sheer frenzy! The cheeks are pale, the lips white with agony, the chin and throat most exquisitely rounded. The figure sits and leans forward in the chair, straining and rigid, cataleptic with horror. The dress is black velvet, a jewel gleams like a flame in the breast, and a golden crucifix smoulders in the shadow of a fold. This is the lady whose image still lives in the old silver mirror. What dire deed could it be which has left its impress there, so that now, in another age, if the spirit of a man be but worn down to it, he may be conscious of its presence?

One other detail: on the left side of the skirt of the black dress was, as I thought at first, a shapeless bunch of white ribbon. Then, as I looked more intently or as the vision defined itself more clearly, I perceived what it was. It was the hand of a man, clenched and knotted in agony, which held on with a convulsive grasp to the fold of the dress. The rest of the crouching figure was a mere vague outline, but that strenuous hand shone clear on the dark background, with a sinister suggestion of tragedy in its frantic clutch. The man is frightened – horribly frightened. That I can clearly discern. What has terrified him so? Why does he grip the woman's dress? The answer lies amongst those moving figures in the background. They have brought danger both to him and to her. The interest of the thing fascinated me. I thought no more of its relation to my own nerves. I stared and stared as if in a theatre. But I could get no further. The mist thinned. There were tumultuous movements in which all the figures were vaguely concerned. Then the mirror was clear once more.

The doctor says I must drop work for a day, and I can afford to do so, for I have made good progress lately. It is quite evident that the visions depend entirely upon my own nervous state, for I sat in front of the mirror for an hour tonight, with no result whatever. My soothing day has chased them away. I wonder whether I shall ever penetrate what they all mean? I examined the mirror this evening under a good light, and, besides the mysterious inscription "Sanc. X. Pal.", I was able to discern some signs of heraldic marks, very faintly visible upon the silver. They must be very ancient, as they are almost obliterated. So far as I could make out, they were three spearheads, two above and one below. I will show them to the doctor when he calls tomorrow.

14th Jan. – Feel perfectly well again, and I intend that nothing else shall stop me until my task in finished. The doctor was shown the marks on the mirror and agreed that they were armorial bearings. He is deeply interested in all that I have told him, and cross-questioned me closely on the details. It amuses me to notice how he is torn in two by conflicting desires – the one that his patient should lose his symptoms, the other that the medium – for so he regards me – should solve this mystery of the past. He advised continued rest, but did not oppose me too violently when I declared that such a thing was out of the question until the ten remaining ledgers have been checked.

17th Jan. – For three nights I have had no experiences – my day of rest has borne fruit. Only a quarter of my task is left, but I must make a forced march, for the lawyers are clamouring for their material. I will give them enough and to spare. I have him fast on a hundred counts. When they realize what a slippery, cunning rascal he is, I should gain some credit from the case. False trading accounts, false balance sheets, dividends drawn from capital, losses written down as profits, suppression of working expenses, manipulation of petty cash – it is a fine record!

18th Jan. – Headaches, nervous twitches, mistiness, fullness of the temples – all the premonitions of trouble, and the trouble came sure enough. And yet my real sorrow is not so much that the vision should come as that it should cease before all is revealed.

But I saw more tonight. The crouching man was as visible as the lady whose gown he clutched. He is a little swarthy fellow, with a black pointed beard. He has a loose gown of damask trimmed with fur. The prevailing tints of his dress are red. What a fright the fellow is in, to be sure! He cowers and shivers and glares back over his shoulder. There is a small knife in his other hand, but he is far too tremulous and cowed to use it. Dimly now I begin to see the figures in the background. Fierce faces, bearded and dark, shape themselves out of the mist. There is one terrible creature, a skeleton of a man, with hollow cheeks and eyes sunk in his head. He also has a knife in his hand. On the right of the woman stands a tall man, very young, with flaxen hair, his face sullen and dour. The beautiful woman looks up at him in appeal. So does the man on the ground. This youth seems to be the arbiter of their fate. The crouching man draws closer and hides himself in the woman's skirts. The tall youth bends and tries to drag her away from him. So much I saw last night before the mirror cleared. Shall I never know what it leads to and whence it comes? It is not a mere imagination, of that I am very sure. Somewhere, sometime, this scene has been acted, and this old mirror has reflected it. But when – where?

20th Jan. – My work draws to a close, and it is time. I feel a tenseness within my brain, a sense of intolerable strain, which warns me that something must give. I have worked myself to the limit. But tonight should be the last night. With a supreme effort I should finish the final ledger and complete the case before I rise from my chair. I will do it. I will.

7th Feb. – I did. My God, what an experience! I hardly know if I am strong enough yet to set it down.

Let me explain in the first instance that I am writing this in Dr Sinclair's private hospital some three weeks after the last entry in my diary. On the night of 20th January my nervous system finally gave way, and I remembered nothing afterwards until I found myself three days ago in this home of rest. And I can rest with a good conscience. My work was done before I went under. My figures are in the solicitors' hands. The hunt is over.

And now I must describe that last night. I had sworn to finish my work, and so intently did I stick to it, though my head was bursting, that I would never look up until the last column had been added. And yet it was fine self-restraint, for all the time I knew that wonderful things were happening in the mirror. Every nerve in my body told me so. If I looked up there was an end of my work. So I did not look up till all was finished. Then, when at last with throbbing temples I threw down my pen and raised my eyes, what a sight was there!

The mirror in its silver frame was like a stage, brilliantly lit, in which a drama was in progress. There was no mist now. The oppression of my nerves had wrought this amazing clarity. Every feature, every movement, was as clear-cut as in life. To think that I, a tired accountant, the most prosaic of mankind, with the account books of a swindling bankrupt before me, should be chosen of all the human race to look upon such a scene!

It was the same scene and the same figures, but the drama had advanced a stage. The tall young man was holding the woman in his arms. She strained away from him and looked up at him with loathing in her face. They had torn the crouching man away from his hold upon the skirt of her dress. A dozen of them were round him – savage men, bearded men. They hacked at him with knives. All seemed to strike him together. Their arms rose and fell. The blood did not flow from him – it squirted. His red dress was dabbled in it. He threw himself this way and that, purple upon crimson, like an over-ripe plum. Still they hacked, and still the jets shot from him. It was horrible – horrible! They dragged him kicking to the door. The woman looked over her shoulder at him and her mouth gaped. I heard nothing, but I knew that she was screaming. And then, whether it was this nerve-racking vision before me, or whether, my task finished, all the overwork of the past weeks came in one crushing weight upon me, the room danced round me, the floor seemed to sink away beneath my feet, and I remembered no more. In the early morning my landlady found me stretched senseless before the silver mirror, but I knew nothing myself until three days ago I awoke in the deep peace of the doctor's nursing home.

9th Feb. – Only today have I told Dr Sinclair my full experience. He had not allowed me to speak of such matters before. He listened with an absorbed interest. "You don't identify this with any well-known scene in history?" he asked, with suspicion in his eyes. I assured him that I knew nothing of history. "Have you no idea whence that mirror came and to whom it once belonged?" he continued. "Have you?" I asked, for he spoke with meaning. "It's incredible," said he, "and yet how else can one explain it? The scenes which you described before suggested it, but now it has gone beyond all range of coincidence. I will bring you some notes in the evening."

Later – He has just left me. Let me set down his words as closely as I can recall them. He began by laying several musty volumes upon my bed.

"These you can consult at your leisure," said he. "I have some notes here which you can confirm. There is not a doubt that what you have seen is the murder of Rizzio by the Scottish nobles in the presence of Mary, which occurred in March 1566.* Your description of the woman is accurate. The high forehead and heavy eyelids combined with great beauty could hardly apply to two women. The tall young man was her husband, Darnley. Rizzio, says the chronicle, 'was dressed in a loose dressing gown of furred damask, with hose of russet velvet'. With one hand he clutched Mary's gown, with the other he held a dagger. Your fierce, hollow-eyed man was Ruthven, who was new-risen from a bed of sickness. Every detail is exact."

"But why to me?" I asked, in bewilderment. "Why of all the human race to me?"

"Because you were in the fit mental state to receive the impression. Because you chanced to own the mirror which gave the impression."

"The mirror! You think, then, that it was Mary's mirror – that it stood in the room where the deed was done?"

"I am convinced that it was Mary's mirror. She had been queen of France.* Her personal property would be stamped with the royal arms. What you took to be three spearheads were really the lilies of France."

"And the inscription?"

"'Sanc. X. Pal.' You can expand it into Sanctae Crucis Palatium. Someone has made a note upon the mirror as to whence it came. It was the Palace of the Holy Cross."

"Holyrood!" I cried.

"Exactly. Your mirror came from Holyrood. You have had one very singular experience, and have escaped. I trust that you will never put yourself into the way of having such another."

The Homecoming

IN THE SPRING OF THE YEAR 528, a small brig used
to run as a passenger boat between Chalcedon on the
Asiatic shore and Constantinople. On the morning in question, which was that of the feast of St George, the vessel was
crowded with excursionists who were bound for the great
city in order to take part in the religious and festive celebra-
tions which marked the festival of the megalomartyr,* one
of the most choice occasions in the whole vast hagiology of
the Eastern Church. The day was fine and the breeze light,
so that the passengers in their holiday mood were able to
enjoy without a qualm the many objects of interest which
marked the approach to the greatest and most beautiful
capital in the world.

On the right, as they sped up the narrow strait, there
stretched the Asiatic shore, sprinkled with white villages
and with numerous villas peeping out from the woods which
adorned it. In front of them, the Prince's Islands, rising as
green as emeralds out of the deep sapphire blue of the Sea
of Marmora, obscured for the moment the view of the capital. As the brig rounded these, the great city burst suddenly

upon their sight, and a murmur of admiration and wonder rose from the crowded deck. Tier above tier it rose, white and glittering, a hundred brazen roofs and gilded statues gleaming in the sun, with high over all the magnificent shining cupola of St Sophia. Seen against a cloudless sky, it was the city of a dream – too delicate, too airily lovely for earth.

In the prow of the small vessel were two travellers of singular appearance. The one was a very beautiful boy, ten or twelve years of age, swarthy, clear-cut, with dark, curling hair and vivacious black eyes, full of intelligence and of the joy of living. The other was an elderly man, gaunt-faced and grey-bearded, whose stern features were lit up by a smile as he observed the excitement and interest with which his young companion viewed the beautiful distant city and the many vessels which thronged the narrow strait.

"See! See!" cried the lad. "Look at the great red ships which sail out from yonder harbour. Surely, your holiness, they are the greatest of all ships in the world."

The old man, who was the abbot of the monastery of St Nicephorus in Antioch, laid his hand upon the boy's shoulder.

"Be wary, Leon, and speak less loudly, for until we have seen your mother we should keep ourselves secret. As to the red galleys, they are indeed as large as any, for they are the Imperial ships of war, which come forth from the harbour of Theodosius.* Round yonder green point is the Golden Horn, where the merchant ships are moored. But now, Leon, if you follow the line of buildings past the great church, you will see a long row of pillars fronting the sea. It marks the Palace of the Caesars."

The boy looked at it with fixed attention. "And my mother is there," he whispered.

"Yes, Leon, your mother the Empress Theodora and her husband the great Justinian* dwell in yonder palace."

The boy looked wistfully up into the old man's face.

"Are you sure, Father Luke, that my mother will indeed be glad to see me?"

The abbot turned away his face to avoid those questioning eyes.

"We cannot tell, Leon. We can only try. If it should prove that there is no place for you, then there is always a welcome among the brethren of St Nicephorus."

"Why did you not tell my mother that we were coming, Father Luke? Why did you not wait until you had her command?"

"At a distance, Leon, it would be easy to refuse you. An Imperial messenger would have stopped us. But when she sees you, Leon – your eyes, so like her own, your face, which carries memories of one whom she loved – then, if there be a woman's heart within her bosom, she will take you into it. They say that the Emperor can refuse her nothing. They have no child of their own. There is a great future before you, Leon. When it comes, do not forget the poor brethren of St Nicephorus, who took you in when you had no friend in the world."

The old abbot spoke cheerily, but it was easy to see from his anxious countenance that the nearer he came to the capital the more doubtful did his errand appear. What had seemed easy and natural from the quiet cloisters of Antioch became dubious and dark now that the golden domes of Constantinople glittered so close at hand. Ten years before, a wretched woman, whose very name was an offence throughout the eastern world, where she was as infamous for her dishonour as famous for her beauty, had come to the monastery gate, and had persuaded the monks to take charge of her infant son, the child of her shame. There he had been ever since. But she, Theodora, the harlot, returning to the capital, had by the strangest turn of Fortune's wheel caught the fancy and finally the enduring love of Justinian, the heir to the throne. Then on the death of his uncle Justin, the young man had become the greatest monarch upon the earth, and had raised Theodora to be not only his wife and empress, but to be absolute ruler with powers equal to and independent of his own. And she, the polluted one, had risen to the dignity, had cut herself sternly away from all that related to her past life, and had shown signs already of being a great queen, stronger and wiser than her husband, but fierce, vindictive and unbending, a firm support to her friends, but a terror to her foes. This was the woman to whom the Abbot Luke of Antioch was bringing Leon, her forgotten son. If ever her mind strayed back to the days when, abandoned by her lover Ecebolus, the governor of the African Pentapolis, she had made her way on foot through Asia Minor, and left her infant with the monks, it was only to persuade herself that the brethren cloistered far from the world would never identify Theodora the Empress with Theodora the dissolute wanderer, and that the fruits of her sin would be for ever concealed from her Imperial husband.

The little brig had now rounded the point of the Acropolis, and the long blue stretch of the Golden Horn lay before it. The high wall of Theodosius lined the whole harbour, but a narrow verge of land had been left between it and the water's edge to serve as a quay. The vessel ran alongside near the Neorion Gate, and the passengers, after a short scrutiny from the group of helmeted guards who lounged beside it, were allowed to pass through into the great city.

The abbot, who had made several visits to Constantinople upon the business of his monastery, walked with the assured step of one who knows his ground; while the boy, alarmed and yet pleased by the rush of people, the roar and clatter of passing chariots and the vista of magnificent buildings, held tightly to the loose gown of his guide, while staring eagerly about him in every direction. Passing through the steep and narrow streets which led up from the water, they emerged into the open space which surrounds the magnificent pile of St Sophia, the great church begun by Constantine, hallowed by St Chrysostom, and now the seat of the Patriarch,* and the very centre of the Eastern Church. Only with many crossings and genuflections did the pious abbot succeed in passing the revered shrine of his religion, and hurried on to his difficult task.

Having passed St Sophia, the two travellers crossed the marble-paved Augusteum,* and saw upon their right the gilded gates of the hippodrome through which a vast crowd of people was pressing, for though the morning had been devoted to the religious ceremony, the afternoon was given over to secular festivities. So great was the rush of the populace that the two strangers had some difficulty in disengaging themselves from the stream and reaching the huge arch of black marble which formed the outer gate of the palace. Within they were fiercely ordered to halt by a gold-crested and magnificent sentinel who laid his shining spear across their breasts until his superior officer should give them permission to pass. The abbot had been warned, however, that all obstacles would give way if he mentioned the name of Basil the eunuch, who acted as chamberlain of the palace and also as Parakimomen – a high office which meant that he slept at the door of the Imperial bedchamber. The charm worked wonderfully, for at the mention of that potent name the Protosphathaire, or Head of the Palace Guards, who chanced to be upon the spot, immediately detached one of his soldiers with instructions to convoy the two strangers into the presence of the chamberlain.

Passing in succession a middle guard and an inner guard, the travellers came at last into the palace proper, and followed their majestic guide from chamber to chamber, each more wonderful than the last. Marbles and gold, velvet and silver, glittering mosaics, wonderful carvings, ivory screens, curtains of Armenian tissue and of Indian silk, damask from Arabia, and amber from the Baltic – all these things merged themselves in the minds of the two simple provincials, until their eyes ached and their senses reeled before the blaze and the glory of this, the most magnificent of the dwellings of man. Finally, a pair of curtains, crusted with gold, were parted, and their guide handed them over to a Negro eunuch who stood within. A heavy, fat, brown-skinned man, with a large, flabby, hairless face, was pacing up and down the small apartment, and he turned upon them as they entered with an abominable and threatening smile. His loose lips and pendulous cheeks were those of a gross old woman, but above them there shone a pair of dark malignant eyes, full of fierce intensity of observation and judgement.

"You have entered the palace by using my name," he said. "It is one of my boasts that any of the populace can approach me in this way. But it is not fortunate for those who take advantage of it without due cause." Again he smiled a smile which made the frightened boy cling tightly to the loose serge skirts of the abbot.

But the ecclesiastic was a man of courage. Undaunted by the sinister appearance of the great chamberlain, or by the threat which lay in his words, he laid his hand upon his young companion's shoulder and faced the eunuch with a confident smile.

"I have no doubt, Your Excellency," said he, "that the importance of my mission has given me the right to enter the palace. The only thing which troubles me is whether it may not be so important as to forbid me from broaching it to you, or indeed, to anybody save the Empress Theodora, since it is she only whom it concerns."

The eunuch's thick eyebrows bunched together over his vicious eyes.

"You must make good those words," he said. "If my gracious master – the ever-glorious Emperor Justinian – does not disdain to take me into his most intimate confidence in all things, it would be strange if there were any subject within your knowledge which I might not hear. You are, as I gather from your garb and bearing, the abbot of some Asiatic monastery?"

"You are right, Your Excellency, I am the abbot of the Monastery of St Nicephorus in Antioch. But I repeat that I am assured that what I have to say is for the ear of the Empress Theodora only."

The eunuch was evidently puzzled, and his curiosity aroused by the old man's persistence. He came nearer, his heavy face thrust forward, his flabby brown hands, like two sponges, resting upon the table of yellow jasper before him.

"Old man," said he, "there is no secret which concerns the Empress which may not be told to me. But if you refuse to speak, it is certain that you will never see her. Why should I admit you, unless I know your errand? How should I know that you are not a Manichean heretic with a poniard in your bosom, longing for the blood of the mother of the Church?"

The abbot hesitated no longer. "If there be a mistake in the matter, then on your head be it," said he. "Know then that this lad Leon is the son of Theodora the Empress, left by her in our monastery within a month of his birth ten years ago. This papyrus which I hand you will show you that what I say is beyond all question or doubt."

The eunuch Basil took the paper, but his eyes were fixed upon the boy, and his features showed a mixture of amazement at the news that he had received, and of cunning speculation as to how he could turn it to profit.

"Indeed, he is the very image of the Empress," he muttered; and then, with sudden suspicion, "Is it not the chance of this likeness which has put the scheme into your head, old man?"

"There is but one way to answer that," said the abbot. "It is to ask the Empress herself whether what I say is not true, and to give her the glad tidings that her boy is alive and well."

The tone of confidence, together with the testimony of the papyrus, and the boy's beautiful face, removed the last shadow of doubt from the eunuch's mind. Here was a great fact; but what use could he make of it? Above all, what advantage could he draw from it? He stood with his fat chin in his hand, turning it over in his cunning brain.

"Old man," said he at last, "to how many have you told this secret?"

"To no one in the whole world," the other answered. "There is Deacon Bardas at the monastery and myself. No one else knows anything."

"You are sure of this?"

"Absolutely certain."

The eunuch had made up his mind. If he alone of all men in the palace knew of this event, he would have a powerful hold over his masterful mistress. He was certain that Justinian the Emperor knew nothing of this. It would be a shock to him. It might even alienate his affections from his wife. She might care to take precautions to prevent him from knowing. And if he, Basil the eunuch, was her confederate in those precautions, then how very close it must draw him to her. All this flashed through his mind as he stood, the papyrus in his hand, looking at the old man and the boy.

"Stay here," said he. "I will be with you again." With a swift rustle of his silken robes he swept from the chamber.

A few minutes had elapsed when a curtain at the end of the room was pushed aside, and the eunuch, reappearing, held it back, doubling his unwieldy body into a profound obeisance as he did so. Through the gap came a small alert woman, clad in golden tissue, with a loose outer mantle and shoes of the Imperial purple. That colour alone showed that she could be none other than the Empress; but the dignity of her carriage, the fierce authority of her magnificent dark eyes, and the perfect beauty of her haughty face, all proclaimed that it could only be that Theodora who, in spite of her lowly origin, was the most majestic as well as the most maturely lovely of all the women in her kingdom. Gone now were the buffoon tricks which the daughter of Acacius the bearward had learnt in the amphitheatre; gone too was the light charm of the wanton, and what was left was the worthy mate of a great king, the measured dignity of one who was every inch an empress.

Disregarding the two men, Theodora walked up to the boy, placed her two white hands upon his shoulders, and looked with a long questioning gaze, a gaze which began with hard suspicion and ended with tender recognition, into those large lustrous eyes which were the very reflection of her own. At first the sensitive lad was chilled by the cold intent question of the look; but as it softened, his own spirit responded, until suddenly, with a cry of "Mother! Mother!" he cast himself into her arms, his hands locked round her neck, his face buried in her bosom. Carried away by the sudden natural outburst of emotion, her own arms tightened round the lad's figure, and she strained him for an instant to her heart. Then, the strength of the Empress gaining instant command over the temporary weakness of the mother, she pushed him back from her, and wanted that they should leave her to herself. The slaves in attendance hurried the two visitors from the room. Basil the eunuch lingered, looking down at his mistress, who had thrown herself upon a damask couch, her lips white and her bosom heaving with the tumult of her emotion. She glanced up and met the chancellor's crafty gaze, her woman's instinct reading the threat that lurked within it.

"I am in your power," she said. "The Emperor must never know of this."

"I am your slave," said the eunuch, with his ambiguous smile. "I am an instrument in your hand. If it is your will that the Emperor should know nothing, then who is to tell him?"

"But the monk, the boy? What are we to do?"

"There is only one way for safety," said the eunuch.

She looked at him with horrified eyes. His spongy hands were pointing down to the floor. There was an underground world to this beautiful palace, a shadow that was ever close to the light, a region of dimly lit passages, of shadowed corners, of noiseless, tongueless slaves, of sudden sharp screams in the darkness. To this the eunuch was pointing.

A terrible struggle rent her breast. The beautiful boy was hers, flesh of her flesh, bone of her bone. She knew it beyond all question or doubt. It was her one child, and her whole heart went out to him. But Justinian! She knew the Emperor's strange limitations. Her career in the past was forgotten. He had swept it all aside by special Imperial decree published throughout the empire, as if she were newborn through the power of his will, and her association with his person. But they were childless, and this sight of one which was not his own would cut him to the quick. He could dismiss her infamous past from his mind, but if it took the concrete shape of this beautiful child, then how could he wave it aside as if it had never been? All her instincts and her intimate knowledge of the man told her that even her charm and her influence might fail under such circumstances to save her from ruin. Her divorce would be as easy to him as her elevation had been. She was balanced upon a giddy pinnacle, the highest in the world, and yet the higher the deeper the fall. Everything that earth could give was now at her feet. Was she to risk the losing of it all – for what? For a weakness which was unworthy of an Empress, for a foolish newborn spasm of love, for that which had no existence within her in the morning? How could she be so foolish as to risk losing such a substance for such a shadow?

"Leave it to me," said the brown watchful face above her.

"Must it be – death?"

"There is no real safety outside. But if your heart is too merciful, then by the loss of sight and speech…"

She saw in her mind the white-hot iron approaching those glorious eyes, and she shuddered at the thought.

"No, no! Better death than that!"

"Let it be death then. You are wise, great Empress, for there only is real safety and assurance of silence."

"And the monk?"

"Him also."

"But the Holy Synod! He is a tonsured priest. What would the Patriarch do?"

"Silence his babbling tongue. Then let them do what they will. How are we of the palace to know that this conspirator, taken with a dagger in his sleeve, is really what he says?"

Again she shuddered and shrank down among the cushions.

"Speak not of it, think not of it," said the eunuch. "Say only that you leave it in my hands. Nay, then, if you cannot say it, do but nod your head, and I take it as your signal."

In that moment there flashed before Theodora's mind a vision of all her enemies, of all those who envied her rise, of all whose hatred and contempt would rise into a clamour of delight could they see the daughter of the bearward hurled down again into that abyss from which she had been dragged. Her face hardened, her lips tightened, her little hands clenched in the agony of her thought.

"Do it!" she said.

In an instant, with a terrible smile, the messenger of death hurried from the room. She groaned aloud, and buried herself yet deeper amid the silken cushions, clutching them frantically with convulsed and twitching hands.

The eunuch wasted no time for, this deed once done, he became – save for some insignificant monk in Asia Minor, whose fate would soon be sealed – the only sharer of Theodora's secret, and therefore the only person who could curb and bend that most imperious nature. Hurrying into the chamber where the visitors were waiting, he gave a sinister signal, only too well known in those iron days. In an instant the black mutes in attendance seized the old man and the boy, pushing them swiftly down a passage and into a meaner portion of the palace, where the heavy smell of luscious cooking proclaimed the neighbourhood of the kitchens. A side corridor led to a heavily barred iron door, and this in turn opened upon a steep flight of stone steps, feebly illuminated by the glimmer of wall lamps. At the head and foot stood a mute sentinel like an ebony statue, and below, along the dusky and forbidding passages from which the cells opened, a succession of niches in the wall were each occupied by a similar guardian. The unfortunate visitors were dragged brutally down a number of stone-flagged and dismal corridors until they descended another long stair which led so deeply into the earth that the damp feeling in the heavy air and the drip of water all round showed that they had come down to the level of the sea. Groans and cries, like those of sick animals, from the various grated doors which they passed showed how many there were who spent their whole lives in this humid and poisonous atmosphere.

At the end of this lowest passage was a door which opened into a single large, vaulted room. It was devoid of furniture, but in the centre was a large and heavy wooden board clamped with iron. This lay upon a rude stone parapet, engraved with inscriptions beyond the wit of the eastern scholars, for this old well dated from a time before the Greeks founded Byzantium, when men of Chaldea and Phoenicia built with huge unmortared blocks, far below the level of the town of Constantine. The door was closed, and the eunuch beckoned to the slaves that they should remove the slab which covered the well of death. The frightened boy screamed and clung to the abbot, who, ashy-pale and trembling, was pleading hard to melt the heart of the ferocious eunuch.

"Surely, surely, you would not slay the innocent boy!" he cried. "What has he done? Was it his fault that he came here? I alone – I and Deacon Bardas – are to blame. Punish us, if someone must indeed be punished. We are old. It is today or tomorrow with us. But he is so young and so beautiful, with all his life before him. Oh, sir! Oh, Your Excellency, you would not have the heart to hurt him!"

He threw himself down and clutched at the eunuch's knees, while the boy sobbed piteously and cast horror-stricken eyes at the black slaves who were tearing the wooden slab from the ancient parapet beneath. The only answer which the chamberlain gave to the frantic pleadings of the abbot was to take a stone which lay on the coping of the well and toss it in. It could be heard clattering against the old, damp, mildewed walls, until it fell with a hollow boom into some far-distant subterranean pool. Then he again motioned with his hands, and the black slaves threw themselves upon the boy and dragged him away from his guardian. So shrill was his clamour that no one heard the approach of the Empress. With a swift rush she had entered the room, and her arms were round her son.

"It shall not be! It cannot be!" she cried. "No, no, my darling! My darling! They shall do you no hurt. I was mad to think of it – mad and wicked to dream of it. Oh, my sweet boy! To think that your mother might have had your blood upon her head!"

The eunuch's brows were gathered together at this failure of his plans, at this fresh example of feminine caprice.

"Why kill them, great lady, if it pains your gracious heart?" said he. "With a knife and a branding iron they can be disarmed for ever."

She paid no attention to his words. "Kiss me, Leon!" she cried. "Just once let me feel my own child's soft lips rest upon mine. Now again! No, no more, or I shall weaken for what I have still to say and still to do. Old man, you are very near a natural grave, and I cannot think from your venerable aspect that words of falsehood would come readily to your lips. You have indeed kept my secret all these years, have you not?"

"I have in very truth, great Empress. I swear to you by St Nicephorus, patron of our house, that save old Deacon Bardas, there is none who knows."

"Then let your lips still be sealed. If you have kept faith in the past, I see no reason why you should be a babbler in the future. And you, Leon" – she bent her wonderful eyes with a strange mixture of sternness and of love upon the boy – "can I trust you? Will you keep a secret which could never help you, but would be the ruin and downfall of your mother?"

"Oh, mother, I would not hurt you! I swear that I will be silent."

"Then I trust you both. Such provision will be made for your monastery and for your own personal comforts as will make you bless the day you came to my palace. Now you may go. I wish never to see you again. If I did, you might find me in a softer mood, or in a harder, and the one would lead to my undoing, the other to yours. But if by whisper or rumour I have reason to think that you have failed me, then you and your monks and your monastery will have such an end as will be a lesson for ever to those who would break faith with their Empress."

"I will never speak," said the old abbot. "Neither will Deacon Bardas; neither will Leon. For all three I can answer. But there are others – these slaves, the chancellor. We may be punished for another's fault."

"Not so," said the Empress, and her eyes were like flints. "These slaves are voiceless; nor have they any means to tell those secrets which they know. As to you, Basil..." She raised her white hand with the same deadly gesture which he had himself used so short a time before. The black slaves were on him like hounds on a stag.

"Oh, my gracious mistress, dear lady, what is this? What is this? You cannot mean it!" he screamed, in his high, cracked voice. "Oh, what have I done? Why should I die?"

"You have turned me against my own. You have goaded me to slay my own son. You have intended to use my secret against me. I read it in your eyes from the first. Cruel, murderous villain, taste the fate which you have yourself given to so many others. This is your doom. I have spoken."

The old man and the boy hurried in horror from the vault. As they glanced back they saw the erect, inflexible, shimmering, gold-clad figure of the Empress. Beyond they had a glimpse of the green-scummed lining of the well, and of the great red open mouth of the eunuch, as he screamed and prayed while every tug of the straining slaves brought him one step nearer to the brink. With their hands over their ears they rushed away, but even so they heard that last woman-like shriek, and then the heavy plunge far down in the dark abysses of the earth.

A Point of Contact

A CURIOUS TRAIN OF THOUGHT is started when one reflects upon those great figures who have trod the stage of this earth, and actually played their parts in the same act, without ever coming face to face, or even knowing of each other's existence. Baber, the Great Mogul, was, for example, overrunning India at the very moment when Hernando Cortez was overrunning Mexico,* and yet the two could never have heard of each other. Or, to take a more supreme example, what could the Emperor Augustus Caesar know of a certain carpenter's shop wherein there worked a dreamy-eyed boy who was destined to change the whole face of the world? It may be, however, that sometimes these great contemporary forces did approach, touch, and separate – each unaware of the true meaning of the other. So it was in the instance which is now narrated.

It was evening in the port of Tyre, some eleven hundred years before the coming of Christ. The city held, at that time, about a quarter of a million of inhabitants, the majority of whom dwelt upon the mainland, where the buildings of the wealthy merchants, each in its own tree-girt garden, extended for seven miles along the coast. The great island, however, from which the town got its name,* lay out some distance from the shore, and contained within its narrow borders the more famous of the temples and public buildings. Of these temples the chief was that of Melmoth, which covered with its long colonnades the greater part of that side of the island which looked down upon the Sidonian port, so called because only twenty miles away the older city of Sidon maintained a constant stream of traffic with its rising offshoot.

Inns were not yet in vogue, but the poorer traveller found his quarters with hospitable citizens, while men of distinction were frequently housed in the annexe of the temples, where the servants of the priests attended to their wants. On that particular evening there stood in the portico of the temple of Melmoth two remarkable figures who were the centre of observation for a considerable fringe of Phoenician idlers. One of these men was clearly by his face and demeanour a great chieftain. His strongly marked features were those of a man who had led an adventurous life, and were suggestive of every virile quality from brave resolve to desperate execution. His broad, high brow and contemplative eyes showed that he was a man of wisdom as well as of valour. He was clad, as became a Greek nobleman of the period, with a pure white linen tunic, a gold-studded belt supporting a short sword, and a purple cloak. The lower legs were bare, and the feet covered by sandals of red leather, while a cap of white cloth was pushed back upon his brown curls, for the heat of the day was past and the evening breeze most welcome.

His companion was a short, thickset man, bull-necked and swarthy, clad in some dusky cloth which gave him a sombre appearance relieved only by the vivid scarlet of his woollen cap. His manner towards his comrade was one of deference, and yet there was in it also something of that freshness and frankness which go with common dangers and a common interest.

"Be not impatient, sire," he was saying. "Give me two days, or three at the most, and we shall make as brave a show at the muster as any. But, indeed, they would smile if they saw us crawl up to Tenedos* with ten missing oars and the mainsail blown into rags."

The other frowned and stamped his foot with anger.

"We should have been there now had it not been for this cursed mischance," said he. "Aeolus* played us a pretty trick when he sent such a blast out of a cloudless sky."

"Well, sire, two of the Cretan galleys foundered, and Trophimes, the pilot, swears that one of the Argos ships was in trouble. Pray Zeus that it was not the galley of Menelaus.* We shall not be the last at the muster."

"It is well that Troy stands a good ten miles from the sea, for if they came out at us with a fleet they might have us at a disadvantage. We had no choice but to come here and refit, yet I shall have no happy hour until I see the white foam from the lash of our oars once more. Go, Seleucas, and speed them all you may."

The officer bowed and departed, while the chieftain stood with his eyes fixed upon his great dismantled galley over which the riggers and carpenters were swarming. Farther out in the roadstead lay eleven other smaller galleys, waiting until their wounded flagship should be ready for them. The sun, as it shone upon them, gleamed upon hundreds of bronze helmets and breastplates, telling of the warlike nature of the errand upon which they were engaged. Save for them the port was filled with bustling merchant ships taking in cargoes or disgorging them upon the quays. At the very feet of the Greek chieftain three broad barges were moored, and gangs of labourers with wooden shovels were heaving out the mussels brought from Dor, destined to supply the famous Tyrian dye works which adorn the most noble of all garments. Beside them was a tin ship from Britain, and the square boxes of that precious metal, so needful for the making of bronze, were being passed from hand to hand to the waiting wagons. The Greek found himself smiling at the uncouth wonder of a Cornishman who had come with his tin, and who was now lost in amazement as he stared at the long colonnades of the Temple of Melmoth and the high front of the Shrine of Ashtaroth behind it. Even as he gazed some of his shipmates passed their hands through his arms and led him along the quay to a wine shop, as being a building much more within his comprehension. The Greek, still smiling, was turning on his heels to return to the temple, when one of the clean-shaven priests of Baal came towards him.

"It is rumoured, sire," said he, "that you are on a very distant and dangerous venture. Indeed, it is well known from the talk of your soldiers what it is that you have on hand."

"It is true," said the Greek, "that we have a hard task before us. But it would have been harder to bide at home and to feel that the honour of a leader of the Argives* had been soiled by this dog from Asia."

"I hear that all Greece has taken up the quarrel."

"Yes, there is not a chief from Thessaly to the Malea who has not called out his men, and there were twelve hundred galleys in the harbour of Aulis."

"It is a great host," said the priest. "But have ye any seers or prophets among ye who can tell what will come to pass?"

"Yes, we had one such, Calchas his name. He has said that for nine years we shall strive, and only on the tenth will the victory come."

"That is but cold comfort," said the priest. "It is, indeed, a great prize which can be worth ten years of a man's life."

"I would give," the Greek answered, "not ten years but all my life if I could but lay proud Ilium* in ashes and carry back Helen to her palace on the hill of Argos."

"I pray Baal, whose priest I am, that you may have good fortune," said the Phoenician. "I have heard that these Trojans are stout soldiers, and that Hector, the son of Priam,* is a mighty leader."

The Greek smiled proudly.

"They must be stout and well led also," said he, "if they can stand the brunt against the long-haired Argives with such captains as Agamemnon, the son of Atreus from golden Mycenae, or Achilles, son of Peleus, with his Myrmidons. But these things are on the knees of the Fates. In the meantime, my friend, I would fain know who these strange people are who come down the street, for their chieftain has the air of one who is made for great deeds."

A tall man clad in a long white robe, with a golden fillet running through his flowing auburn hair, was striding down the street with the free elastic gait of one who has lived an active life in the open. His face was ruddy and noble, with a short, crisp beard covering a strong, square jaw. In his clear blue eyes as he looked at the evening sky and the busy waters beneath him there was something of the exaltation of the poet, while a youth walking beside him and carrying a harp hinted at the graces of music. On the other side of him, however, a second squire bore a brazen shield and a heavy spear, so that his master might never be caught unawares by his enemies. In his train there came a tumultuous rabble of dark, hawk-like men, armed to the teeth, and peering about with covetous eyes at the signs of wealth which lay in profusion around them. They were swarthy as Arabs, and yet they were better clad and better armed than the wild children of the desert.

"They are but barbarians," said the priest. "He is a small king from the mountain parts opposite Philistia, and he comes here because he is building up the town of Jebus, which he means to be his chief city. It is only here that he can find the wood, and stone, and craftsmanship that he desires. The youth with the harp is his son. But I pray you, chief, if you would know what is before you at Troy, to come now into the outer hall of the temple with me, for we have there a famous seer, the prophetess Alaga who is also the priestess of Ashtaroth. It may be that she can do for you what she has done for many others, and send you forth from Tyre in your hollow ships with a better heart than you came."

To the Greeks, who by oracles, omens and auguries were forever prying into the future, such a suggestion was always welcome. The Greek followed the priest to the inner sanctuary, where sat the famous pythoness – a tall, fair woman of middle age, who sat at a stone table upon which was an abacus or tray filled with sand. She held a style of chalcedony, and with this she traced strange lines and curves upon the smooth surface, her chin leaning upon her other hand and her eyes cast down. As the chief and the priest approached her she did not look up, but she quickened the movements of her pencil, so that curve followed curve in quick succession. Then, still with downcast eyes, she spoke in a strange, high, sighing voice like wind amid the trees.

"Who, then, is this who comes to Alaga of Tyre, the handmaiden of great Ashtaroth? Behold I see an island to the west, and an old man who is the father, and the great chief, and his wife, and his son who now waits him at home, being too young for the wars. Is this not true?"

"Yes, maiden, you have said truth," the Greek answered.

"I have had many great ones before me, but none greater than you, for three thousand years from now people will still talk of your bravery and of your wisdom. They will remember also the faithful wife at home, and the name of the old man, your father, and of the boy your son – all will be remembered when the very stones of noble Sidon and royal Tyre are no more."

"Nay, say not so, Alaga!" cried the priest.

"I speak not what I desire but what it is given to me to say. For ten years you will strive, and then you will win, and victory will bring rest to others, but only new troubles to you. Ah!" The prophetess suddenly started in violent surprise, and her hand made ever faster markings on the sand.

"What is it that ails you, Alaga?" asked the priest.

The woman had looked up with wild enquiring eyes. Her gaze was neither for the priest nor for the chief, but shot past them to the farther door. Looking round the Greek was aware that two new figures had entered the room. They were the ruddy barbarian whom he had marked in the street, together with the youth who bore his harp.

"It is a marvel upon marvels that two such should enter my chamber on the same day," cried the priestess. "Have I not said that you were the greatest that ever came, and yet behold here is already one who is greater. For he and his son – even this youth whom I see before me – will also be in the minds of all men when lands beyond the Pillars of Hercules shall have taken the place of Phoenicia and of Greece. Hail to you, stranger, hail! Pass on to your work for it awaits you, and it is great beyond words of mine." Rising from her stool the woman dropped her pencil upon the sand and passed swiftly from the room.

"It is over," said the priest. "Never have I heard her speak such words."

The Greek chief looked with interest at the barbarian. "You speak Greek?" he asked.

173

"Indifferently well," said the other. "Yet I should understand it seeing that I spent a long year at Ziklag in the land of the Philistines.'

"It would seem," said the Greek, "that the gods have chosen us both to play a part in the world."

"Stranger," the barbarian answered, "there is but one God."

"Say you so? Well, it is a matter to be argued at some better time. But I would fain have your name and style and what is it you purpose to do, so that we may perchance hear of each other in years to come. For my part I am Odysseus, known also as Ulysses, the King of Ithaca, with the good Laertes as my father and young Telemachus as my son. For my work, it is the taking of Troy."

"And my work," said the barbarian, "is the building of Jebus, which now we call Jerusalem. Our ways lie separate, but it may come back to your memory that you have crossed the path of David, second King of the Hebrews, together with his young son Solomon, who may follow him upon the throne of Israel."

So he turned and went forth into the darkened streets where his spearmen were awaiting him, while the Greek passed down to his boat that he might see what was still to be done ere he could set forth upon his voyage.

Note on the Text

The text in the present edition is based on the first edition of *Tales of Long Ago* (1922), a collection of previously published stories. The spelling and punctuation have been standardized, modernized and made consistent throughout.

Notes

p. 5, *Portus Dubris*: Present-day Dover, on the south coast of the island of Great Britain.

p. 5, *Wall of Hadrian*: A defensive fortification extending from coast to coast in northern Britain, built by the Romans under the Emperor Hadrian (AD 76–138), beginning in AD 122.

p. 5, *Camboricum*: Usually identified with Cambridge.

p. 5, *Silures*: A tribe of ancient Britons from what is now South Wales.

p. 6, *Vinovia*: A Roman fort near present-day Bishop Auckland, in the north-east of England.

p. 6, *Icenian*: The name of a tribe from the eastern area of England that is now Norfolk.

p. 7, *bracæ*: "Trousers" (Latin).

p. 8, *the land of Ham*: The reference here is unknown. The Old Testament refers to Egypt as "the land of Ham", but it is unclear why the ancient Britons would claim to have originated in that part of the world. The ninth-century *Anglo-Saxon Chronicle* states that the Britons came from Armenia, which is often assumed to be an incorrect transcription of the name Armorica (modern-day Brittany) – it could be that Doyle intended "Ham" as a plausibly archaic-sounding version of either name.

p. 9, *the Picts*: An ancient people from what is now northern Scotland.

p. 9, *Count of the Saxon Shore*: The head of the Roman military command consisting of a series of fortifications on both sides of the English Channel. The name refers to the Saxons, a Germanic tribe who raided the English coast from the mid-third century.

p. 11, *Anderida*: A Roman fort on the south coast of England.

p. 11, *Northmen*: That is, raiders from Scandinavia; Vikings.

p. 12, *Via Aurelia on their way to the Ligurian passes*: The Via Aurelia was a road beginning in Rome and heading north into the Ligurian Alps.

p. 12, *Caistor*: A Roman fort in what is now Lincolnshire.

p. 12, *Isca*: A Roman fortress and settlement near modern-day Newport in South Wales.

p. 12, *Vectis*: The Roman name for the Isle of Wight, off the south coast of Great Britain.

p. 15, *Mutato nomine, de te, Britannia, fabula narratur*: "Change the name, Britannia, and the story is about you" (Latin). A quotation from the Roman poet Horace (65–8 BC).

p. 15, *Carthage*: The Carthaginian Empire, which controlled the northern coast of Africa and parts of the western Mediterranean, fought a series of wars, known as the Punic Wars, with Rome between 264 and 146 BC. The city of Carthage itself was in modern-day Tunisia.

p. 15, *Tyrian purple*: A crimson dye obtained from certain sea snails and highly prized in the ancient world. It was named after the Phoenician port of Tyre, in present-day Lebanon, from where it came.

p. 18, *the Queen of the Waters*: The Phoenician port of Tyre is described as such in the poem 'The Spirit of Navigation and Discovery' by the English poet and priest William Lisle Bowles (1762–1850).

p. 19, *Tin Islands*: Otherwise known as the Cassiterides, islands believed to lie off the western coast of Europe, and traditionally understood to refer to the British Isles.

p. 22, *Megara*: A suburb of Carthage.

p. 23, *Kabyle*: A member of a Berber people from present-day Algeria.

p. 23, *Punic*: Carthaginian.

p. 24, *Ostia*: The harbour of ancient Rome.

p. 27, *Borderer*: That is, an inhabitant of the Borders region in southern Scotland.

p. 29, *thole*: "Endure" (dialect).

p. 29, *lugs*: "Ears" (dialect).

p. 29, *fosse*: A ditch or excavation.

p. 30, *Valeria Victrix*: The last two words of the name "Legio Vigesima Valeria Victrix", a Roman legion that took part in the invasion of Britain in 43 and stayed there until the fourth century. The exact meaning of the name is disputed; possibilities include: "Twentieth Victorious Valerian Legion" (i.e. from the Roman province of Valeria), "Twentieth Victorious and Valiant Legion" and "Twentieth Legion of the Victorious Black Eagle".

p. 38, *Donatists*: Named after their leader Donatus (d. *c.* AD 355), a schismatic Christian sect that broke away from the Roman Catholic Church in 311 and that flourished until the seventh century.

p. 38, *argument of the Catholic and the Arian*: A reference to the Arian controversy, a series of disputes within the Church during the fourth century concerning the heretical beliefs of Arius (*c.* AD 250–*c.*336), an Alexandrian priest, who denied the divinity of Christ on the basis that the Son, as a creation of the Father, cannot be coeternal with the Father, or of the same substance.

p. 38, *the Homoousian and of the Homoiousian*: Two similar but distinct theological positions adopted by some during the Arian controversy. The Homoousians believed that the Son was of the same substance as the Father, whereas the Homoiousians believed that the Son was of a similar but not identical substance.

p. 38, *Pontus*: A region in Asia Minor on the southern coast of the Black Sea.

p. 39, *Athanasius*: St Athanasius (*c.* AD 293–373), the chief defender of Church orthodoxy during the Arian controversy.

p. 39, *the Dniester*: A river beginning in the Carpathians and ending at the Black Sea.

p. 41, *Tyras*: On the northern coast of the Black Sea.

p. 41, *the Logos*: The Word of God, identified with Christ. See John 1:1.

p. 43, *the book which was written by our Emperor Marcus Aurelius*: The Roman Emperor Marcus Aurelius (AD 121–80) was the author of a book of reflections on Stoic philosophy, known as *Meditations*.

p. 43, *the words and actions of our late Emperor Julian*: The Roman Emperor Julian (*c.* AD 331–63) was a philosopher and author. He attempted to restore paganism to Rome, following the conversion of the empire to Christianity in 324 under his uncle, the Emperor Constantine (*c*. AD 274–337).

p. 49, *since Constantine had moved the capital of the world to the shores of the Bosphorus*: In 330, the Emperor Constantine made Byzantium the capital of the empire, renaming it Constantinople.

p. 55, *the most singular design that any monarch has ever entertained*: The Emperor Nero (AD 37–68) competed in the Olympic Games in 67, taking part both in a chariot race and in acting and singing competitions.

p. 55, *Puteoli*: Modern-day Pozzuoli, near Naples on the western coast of Italy.

p. 67, *Ex ovo omnia*: "All life comes from an egg" (Latin). From Ovid's *Metamorphoses*.

p. 67, *the Georgics*: A collection of four poems on the subject of agriculture by the Roman poet Virgil (70–19 BC).

p. 68, *Vortigern*: A semi-legendary fifth-century king of the Britons.

p. 69, *Venta*: Either Venta Belgarum, the Roman name for Winchester, or a river and a town of this name in Lithuania. (The latter is consistent with the author of the letter's earlier reference to voyages to the Baltic.)

p. 71, *Tacitus has remarked upon this characteristic of the Germans*: The Roman historian Tacitus (*c.* AD 56–120) was the author of the *Germania* (AD 98), an ethnographic about the Germanic tribes.

p. 72, *Woden*: The supreme god in Norse, and wider Germanic, mythology, also known as Odin.

p. 76, *Gracchus*: Tiberius Sempronius Gracchus (*c.*160–*c.*133 BC), a Roman politician who reformed agricultural legislation in an attempt to transfer wealth and power from the landowning nobility to the poor.

p. 79, *Semita Alta*: The Alta Semita ("high path"), a street in ancient Rome.

p. 79, *the Emperor Domitian*: Domitian (AD 51–96), Roman Emperor from 81 to 96.

p. 80, *cannot say of him… beggared the empire*: Vitellius (AD 15–69) was the third of the short-lived emperors who followed the suicide of Nero in 68, ruling for eight months in the year 69 (the "Year of the Four Emperors"). He was renowned for his gluttony.

p. 80, *the year that Titus took Jerusalem*: Jerusalem, which had been seized in a Jewish rebellion in 66, was besieged and recaptured by the Romans under the future Emperor Titus (AD 39–81) in the year 70.

p. 81, *ordinarii*: "Overseers" (Latin). The intended meaning here appears to be something like "servants".

p. 82, *ergastulum*: A prison or dungeon in which slave workers were held.

p. 82, *The Greek Venus of Praxiteles*: The Greek sculptor Praxiteles, who lived in the fourth century BC, was best known for a statue of Aphrodite (known to the Romans as Venus), of which only copies survive.

p. 82, *Pentelic marble*: Mount Pentelicus in Attica, Greece, was renowned for its marble.

p. 84, *catenæ*: "Chains" (Latin).

p. 85, *furca*: An instrument of torture resembling a yoke and shaped like a fork.

p. 85, *datura*: A poisonous flower.

p. 91, *Thrace*: An ancient region comprising modern Bulgaria and parts of Turkey.

p. 92, *the Alani*: A nomadic people who lived in the steppe region to the north of the Black Sea.

p. 92, *turmæ*: "Cavalry squadrons" (Latin).

p. 92, *the Emperor Septimius Severus*: Septimius Severus (AD 146–211), Roman Emperor AD 193–211.

p. 94, *decurions*: Officers in charge of *turmæ*.

p. 95, *sloping vallum and gaping fossa*: Respectively the wall of a Roman fortification and the surrounding trench.

p. 102, *Severus Alexander*: Severus Alexander (AD 208–35), Roman Emperor from AD 222 to 235.

p. 104, *the African Pentapolis*: Cyrenaica, the eastern coastal region of Libya.

p. 109, *the soldier Emperor*: Maximinus I, also known as Maximinus Thrax (*c.* AD 173–238), originally a shepherd from Thrace, was the first of the "soldier emperors", that is, soldiers who achieved the office after rising through the ranks. Soldier emperors were especially common during the period of instability for the empire known as the "Crisis of the Third Century".

p. 115, *Emperor Maurice*: Maurice (539–602), Byzantine (or "Eastern Roman") Emperor 582–602.

p. 116, *the Pillars of Hercules*: Two promontories on either side of the Strait of Gibraltar.

p. 117, *Macoraba*: Mecca.

p. 118, *shouted for the Green at the hippodrome*: There were two major chariot-racing "teams" in the Byzantine Empire, the Blues and the Greens.

p. 122, *the Koraish*: The Koraish, or Quraysh, were a powerful tribe that ruled Mecca and its Kaaba shrine at the time of the birth of the Prophet Muhammad (*c.*570–632).

p. 123, *the Caaba*: The Caaba, or Kaaba, is an ancient Meccan shrine believed to have been built by Abraham, which is now at the centre of the Great Mosque and held by Muslims to be the most sacred place on earth.

p. 125, *themes*: A "theme" was an administrative division of the Byzantine Empire.

p. 143, *the murder of Rizzio... in March 1566*: David Rizzio (*c.*1533–66), was an Italian courtier and the private secretary of Mary, Queen of Scots (1542–87). Mary's second husband, Henry Stuart, Lord Darnley (1545–67), grew jealous of Rizzio, believing that he had made Mary pregnant, and so joined a conspiracy of Protestant nobles, led by Patrick Ruthven, 3rd Lord Ruthven (*c.*1520–66), to have him killed.

p. 143, *She had been queen of France*: Mary's first husband was Francis I of France, whom she married when he was still dauphin in 1568. He ascended to the throne the following year, but died in December 1560, after which Mary returned to Scotland.

p. 145, *megalomartyr*: In the Eastern Orthodox Church, certain saints (including St George) are revered as "megalomartyrs", meaning "great martyrs".

p. 147, *the harbour of Theodosius*: One of the ports of Constantinople, named after Theodosius I (AD 347–95), Roman Emperor from 379 to 395.

p. 147, *the Empress Theodora and her husband the great Justinian*: Justinian I (*c.*482–565), known as Justinian the Great, was Byzantine Emperor from 527 to 565. He is famous for attempting to reconquer the Western Roman

Empire (which fell in the late fifth century) and for codifying Roman law. His wife Theodora (*c*.497–548), a former courtesan, was extremely powerful and influential on the policies of her husband.

p. 150, *the Patriarch*: The Ecumenical Patriarch, the highest-ranking bishop of the Orthodox Church.

p. 150, *Augusteum*: A temple devoted to the cult of the Emperor.

p. 165, *Baber, the Great Mogul... Hernando Cortez was overrunning Mexico*: Babur (1483–1530), a descendant of the Mongol conqueror Tamerlane (1336–1405), invaded India in around 1525 and became the first Mogul emperor (*c*.1525–30). Hernán Cortés (1485–1547) was the first of the conquistadors, the sixteenth-century Spanish conquerors of Peru and Mexico. Between 1519 and 1521, he overthrew the Aztec empire, destroying its capital, Tenochtitlán, and toppling its emperor, Montezuma.

p. 166, *The great island, however, from which the town got its name*: The Phoenician port of Tyre was built on an offshore island, and relied on the neighbouring urban centre of Ushu on the mainland for drinking water and raw materials.

p. 167, *Tenedos*: A Turkish island in the Aegean, directly opposite the ancient city of Troy.

p. 167, *Aeolus*: The Greek god of the winds.

p. 167, *Menelaus*: As related in Homer's *Iliad*, it was the abduction of Helen, wife of Menelaus, king of Sparta, by the Trojan prince Paris that triggered the Trojan war.

p. 169, *a leader of the Argives*: The Argives were the inhabitants of the Greek city-state of Argos. However, since Menelaus was king of Sparta, the rival of Argos, it is clear that, like Homer, Doyle is using the term to refer to the Greeks in general.

p. 170, *Ilium*: Another name for Troy.

p. 170, *Priam*: King of Troy.

ALMA CLASSICS

ALMA CLASSICS aims to publish mainstream and lesser-known European classics in an innovative and striking way, while employing the highest editorial and production standards. By way of a unique approach the range offers much more, both visually and textually, than readers have come to expect from contemporary classics publishing.

To order any of our titles and for up-to-date information about our current and forthcoming publications, please visit our website on:

www.almaclassics.com